A Place Called Why

A Novel

Nabila Altaf

Copyright © 2023 Nabila Altaf
All rights reserved
First Edition

NEWMAN SPRINGS PUBLISHING
320 Broad Street
Red Bank, NJ 07701

First originally published by Newman Springs Publishing 2023

This is a work of Literary Fiction. Any resemblance to persons or places are purely coincidental and based on the author's own imagination.

ISBN 979-8-88763-771-6 (Paperback)
ISBN 979-8-88763-772-3 (Digital)

Printed in the United States of America

To my father, who showed me the world

Prologue

PESHAWAR 1965

The jungle, the woods, the forest animals—all came as part and parcel of the universe that was now his center. It was unimportant to him how he got here. He remained aware and yet completely oblivious to these surroundings. His mind and heart were sifting through the noise and urgency of the last forty-two years of his life. The strong and disciplined teachings of his father, the tutors, and then the rigorous curriculum at school and university—all began to take on a new light. Teaching engineering at the college, he became very popular and was promoted over the years, finally to vice-chancellor of the Engineering Department last year.

His hunger for success and need for power were satiated by the accolades and prestige that these positions provided.

It has been, from what he could surmise, about nine months since he left the comfort of his home in Peshawar. His books were scattered in the study as he walked out the door of his home, and his wife had gone to the market. She had been showing signs of concern toward him lately. He would not come out of his study, even for meals. He would just ask, very sporadically, for a cup of chai or a glass of water. Sleeping on the floor, depleted, he would stay up into the late hours of the night and, many times, until the slow rise of dawn. He had been restless in those last few months, studying all the works of the great thinkers, searching for something. Socrates, Plato, Rumi, Allama Iqbal, Confucius, Carl Jung, Nietzsche, and Kierkegaard were swimming like schools of fish, convening in an ocean of knowledge and floating onto the life raft that was his mind. This myriad of ideas, where great thoughts and philosophies converged, overlapped and was profoundly definitive, yet something was missing.

His search continued, and he then went on to the books. Ah yes, the books. He was raised on the text of the Holy Quran, the belief of a one true and great God, his prophets, and the miracles. That core belief had not changed, but he had eventually evolved from the basics. All the reading and learning had left a burning desire in him to solve the mystery. He felt that, although many observed their religions and philosophies with great conviction, few understood the central place of God's presence in their lives, of his love and what it meant. Some refused to acknowledge this existence at all, as the agnostics and atheists do, and others followed blindly and without question. The Bible, the Torah, the Bhagavat Gita, and other ancient texts—all espoused the greatness of God and his fury, his mercy. But the love was some ethereal mystery that man had to decipher under the writing and the layers. Where there was the love, there was God; this he knew. Perhaps love was the absence of fear, and fear was what man used to create an organized structure to control the human race.

The man's adherence to his daily prayers and meditations remained steadfast as his days on this odyssey continued. Whether ritualistic or spiritual, these helped him maintain his connection to God, which he felt increasingly more as the time passed. He would walk for hours, then rest and pray. He found water by the small creeks to wash with and do his ablutions; a remaining cloth from his clothes was also washed and laid out for his prayer rug. He could eat the berries and fruit on some of the trees, but surprisingly, he did not feel hunger, thirst, pain, or lack of energy.

Time is moving, and yet we stand still, he thought. If stillness is a sign of peace, then he was at peace.

His once crisp cotton shirt and pajama were now worn down to shreds. He finally ripped off the nubby seams and wrapped the remaining cloth around his midsection like a loincloth. There was none or very little visible fat left on him. His skin clung tightly to his bones as he sat quietly under the banyan tree.

A few times, some passersby would see him, hunters or thieves cutting through the dense forest on their way to another destination. They would be startled at first, and then, maybe feeling sorry for him, they would throw a piece of bread or a fruit in his lap. A few larger animals would circle around him, thinking about a good meal perhaps, but then they would slowly wander off in another direction.

Once, he wandered out closer to the edge of the forest, where he could see the sunrise more clearly. A group of young boys were running and laughing loudly when they came across him seated under a tree, and they suddenly stopped. They started making fun of his skimpy attire, wild hair, and long beard. They started calling him names.

"Hey, monkey man! Go back into the jungle," one boy shouted.

They guffawed and roared with laughter, and another called out, "Ya. Go get some clothes on, you stinky monkey man!"

When he did not flinch or open his eyes, they started throwing stones at him. His eyes were closed, but his mind was still very lucid from his morning meditation. When one stone hit him on the left side of his forehead, his eyes jolted open. He did not feel the pain, but he did sense the blood trickling on his forehead. He placed his hand there to see the bright red fluid smeared on his fingers.

Something inside him began to churn, a strange burning and twisting in his chest. He closed his eyes, trying to calm it down, but then it just popped out of him, whirling through his diaphragm and out of his mouth with a fierce "Ghaah!" As he looked up at the group of laughing boys, his eyes fixed on the largest boy, who was also the loudest and the one that had thrown the rock at his head. He knew that somehow. Suddenly, the boy reeled back, as if being slapped or punched in the face, and he fell hard to the ground. He was holding his head as the other boys surrounded him.

"What happened, Ali? Are you all right?"

Ali just stared at the strange bony man sitting by the tree, whose eyes were transfixed on him.

"How did you do that?" he demanded. "What are you? Speak to me!" His voice became loud and belligerent, but the man did not move.

In a soft and gentle voice, the man said, "Come here, my boy." He gestured to Ali.

The boy stood up, defiant, rubbing his face from the impact of whatever it was that hit him. "No!" he shouted. "We are getting out of here. This guy is some kind of *jadu* shit. Come on, guys. *Chalo!*"

The man replied to this in an even softer voice, almost a hush, so that the boys had to bend forward to listen. He addressed Ali specifically as his eyes locked with the angry young boy's. "Suit yourself. But the next time you harm a helpless soul, that mark where you were hit will turn a bright shade of red… unless you listen to what I have to say."

This warning had no effect on the boy, and he hastily led the others away, charging out of the forest at lightning speed.

Many years later, tales spread of a madman in a white loincloth wandering the jungles. He would suddenly appear at the mosque in the village and sometimes simultaneously at a well nearly thirty miles north. These tales would cause curious gossip and murmurings among the small towns and villages. There were few who would believe, but on the most part, they thought him mad.

The man knew then that his forest days were over. He had reached a level of understanding that allowed him to feel and decipher the deeper meaning of God's grace and love. He felt protected and strong, both physically and spiritually.

On his last night, he washed and then prayed for many hours until the sound of crickets and the running stream finally coerced him to lay his head down. The face of Abdul Baba—one of the great saints who had mentored him in his early days at Aligarh University—appeared in a dream and smiled at him. There was a white glow surrounding his head, and he looked at the man with an intensity that filled him with warmth. Abdul Baba was one of the great healers and enlightened Sufis that he had met and had many interactions with in the last few years. The man became his *mureed*, or follower.

Abdul Baba held his hand and led him through the forest until there was a clearing, and a large green mountain was visible against the bright blue sky. "You see that mountain ahead?" He pointed in the distance. "There is a trail there, carved in the shape of a *Y*, in the center of the *Y* on that mountain. Do you see it?"

The man was not sure if he had to reply but just acknowledged the gesture with a nod.

"This is where you will build it. You will create a place of peace and unity, where all will gather to hear what you have learned. You must share your knowledge. Knowledge and love are like fruits in a beautiful cupboard. If they are not taken out and shared, they will rot, and no one will be the better."

They walked around the area for a while in silence, and the man said that he understood. A warm breeze drifted around them suddenly, and Abdul Baba was gone. The man looked around and just saw the mountain with the *Y* carved deeply on it and in his mind.

Upon waking up, he felt refreshed and full of a lightness that he had never felt before. It was time to go home.

Sahil

BOSTON, MASSACHUSETTS
(2015)

The semester was almost over. *Thank God*, Sahil thought to himself. It was true that he enjoyed the assistant professor position, teaching, and all its advantages here at the university, but this left very little time for research or any opportunity to decompress. The hierarchy here was understood and undeterred. The tenured professors expected the newbie teachers to carry the class, grade the papers, and put in time to help them with their research. He knew this professorship was a golden opportunity, especially for someone his age. And the fact was that he was in his element and loved every minute of it. He also knew that there were many who would kill for such an opportunity, so complaining was not an option.

But this did not discount the fact that he was completely overworked and exhausted. The one saving grace that he had to look forward to was his trip back home. For a few weeks, he would get to see his family and then enjoy the respite in the Swat Valley at the peaceful retreat nestled in those green hills. The image in his mind of the lush mountains, clear pools of spring water, home-cooked food, and the warmth and laughter of his close friends and family calmed his thoughts and helped him focus on the day ahead.

He strode briskly from the small musty office space that served as his incubator since he arrived here. He was glad to see that the hot summer weather had not descended on the campus just yet. A cool springlike breeze drifted in the air this morning, so his fifteen-minute walk from the faculty offices to the lecture hall was invigorating.

A nice cup of hot tea would be perfect right now, he thought as skipping breakfast or his morning tea routine had become a habit lately. The papers had to be finished and the final exams graded. The American lust for coffee had still not seduced him. The faculty mostly drank it black, which was intolerable, or the local coffee shops had so many concoctions of the drink that it seemed more trouble than a beverage deserved. A well-brewed cup of Darjeeling tea with steamed milk and some sugar had always been a simple pleasure that he looked forward to. He still did not understand how some people can take hot water in a Styrofoam cup, drop a tea bag in it, and call it a cup of tea.

As he entered the lecture hall, the seats were starting to fill up, and he had to pass out the exams and go over the results.

"Here is your tea, Sahil," a clear and sharp voice echoed next to him.

He looked up from the papers to see his assistant, Kim, putting a white porcelain mug of hot caramel-colored tea next to his papers. Kim had been hired on his insistence that, in order for him to finish his doctorate thesis on time and teach, he would need some admin support. He was actually surprised when the dean caved in and agreed to hire someone temporarily four months ago. Since the university was paying for his education and his salary, it was obvious that the sooner he finished, the less of a financial burden it was to them.

She was chosen from a round of 356 applicants. The assistant's salary was not much, but it would benefit Kim immensely when applying for her doctorate. The fact that she was quite attractive did not hurt her chances, he assumed, although he could be wrong about this. The dean had been known to be biased to the pretty undergrads that showed up at his office quite often. He had to check himself from time to time to not let his patriarchal and cultural bias affect his rational thinking.

She was a highly intelligent, coolheaded young woman who took on more than her share of work without ever complaining. Her short blond hair was cropped around a small and angled head, and her piercing blue eyes missed nothing. She reminded him of a sleek jungle animal, hunting for prey or at least wary of such. This detached nature in the academic world displayed by women here was new to him. The women he knew and grew up with were so emotionally charged with such strong opinions that his paradigm of women had expanded and evolved unbelievably in the last four years since his arrival here in the US.

He quickly looked up at her. "You read my mind, Kim. Thank you!"

She gave him a quick smile. "I knew that today was going to be crazy. And as usual, you don't bother to make your tea anymore." She said this with a familiarity that he had started noticing lately.

Her obvious interest in him was both flattering and daunting, and it didn't take a rocket scientist to figure that one out. Even a nuclear scientist like himself could read the signals. She came to his office after hours often to go over the coursework or get help on a certain project, lingering and making small talk. These small attempts at forming some kind of a connection may have been harmless, but he knew that any relationship in his life right now would take a back seat to his career. Unfortunately though, overthinking and analyzing problems to a pulp had always been one of his greatest flaws. To commit to the demands that a romantic relationship required would be out of the question, although something told him that a relationship with her would be a low-maintenance one. Nevertheless, going on dates, giving undivided attention, and remembering birthdays, anniversaries, and the like could take up a huge amount of time—a luxury that he seriously could not afford right now.

Having grown up in a household of sisters and aunts, he knew that the female species was not one to be taken lightly. His world was defined by the fact that any woman worth knowing was a force to be dealt with, and whomever he decided to bring into his life, it would be for the long haul. He couldn't understand all the lightweight sleeping around that was commonplace on campus. Even professors with students: it didn't make sense to him. It seemed like a waste of energy and time. His point of view, he realized, was partly cultural, partly based on values, and mostly because he was wary of getting in over his head with a girl who did not know where he came from, much less where he was going. Perhaps he was still searching for his own identity, and he needed that to be clear before he could let another person into his world. Or just maybe he hadn't clicked with anyone to that extent yet.

Again with the overthinking. *Stop it!* His inner voice needed to back down. Besides, he knew that once he finished here, Ammi would be scouting around for suitable girls to match him up with and probably already had. Not that he wouldn't have a say in the matter. Getting to know the "prospective bride" would be critical, but the initial screening process was usually done by the mothers and sisters.

It's a strange dilemma, this whole traditional approach to marriage. On the one hand, there are so many opportunities to meet a partner, and yet, on the other hand, what guarantee do we have in life that we find the perfect human being to share a lifetime with? After all, his parents did not even meet until the wedding day, and they had forty-two years together, stable and seemingly happy. He should ask his mother about this some time; it might be an interesting subject to approach with her.

After handing back all the papers, he looked up to see a medley of groans and smiles along with the protests for which he knew there would be some after-hours meetings set up. It was always inevitable in academia that nothing was ever finite. But in this case, he needed to set that clarity. Engineering and science had no gray areas, despite what these kids thought. He had nothing to prove him otherwise. It was an easy approach to a complex problem; this was how problems were solved.

"Well, another semester done. Seems that the students have done really well, don't you think, Sahil?" She was in his office, perched on one of the side tables near his desk as he straightened out the papers and put away the files to keep some order when he returned from his trip.

"Yes. It has been tougher for some of them than others, but the ones that stay with it and work hard, they will do well." He started to get up to retrieve his backpack from the floor when he remembered something that he wanted to ask her. "Hey, Kim. By the way, have you any more info about the new TA here, the guy from Afghanistan who applied for his doctorate? He has been hanging around a lot and asking so many questions. His English is pretty good, so he probably studied abroad. But there's just something about him that I can't put a finger on. Something that seems odd."

She looked over at him and smiled. "You are always so suspicious. Honestly, he just wants to get to know everyone in the department. I think he seems really nice."

"Oh, okay." Sahil knew that Kim was a sharp cookie, and keeping good relations with all the top-tier faculty would be to her advantage. She was going to go far in this university, he thought. He just didn't have the bandwidth to deal with such strategies and politics, though he could probably learn a few things from her, if he was so inclined.

"Well, that about takes care of things on my end," he said. "You are sure you will be okay for the summer term? I know it's only two classes, but hopefully, the seats are not filled up."

"Yeah, sure. Don't worry about anything. I can always email you if there's an issue. You go and enjoy your time with your family in Pakistan."

"Thanks, Kim. The other faculty members are also around most of the summer, so it should be fine. I will have my laptop and papers with me since I still have to finish up some loose ends on my dissertation, so no worries."

He gave her a smile, and she approached him and gave a friendly hug. "See you when you get back, Dr. Khan!"

Dr. Khan, Sahil thought. It sounded good, but something in her voice was almost sarcastic. He needed to stop imagining stupid nuances in everything and focus on his work and get packed up to leave for the airport.

Just as he was about to exit his office, another student showed up, wanting to discuss his final grade.

"I can take care of this," Kim reassured him.

But this was his student, and he knew the guy had been struggling. "It's fine, Kim. You go. I will see what he is upset about."

The flights abroad were always late at night, so this suited his schedule well.

The last student was shoved out of his office by early evening, and he rushed back to his apartment to finish packing so he could leave before it got too late. He knew that he should have taken a stronger stand, but the student was from India. He was smart but not very studious. His family had money, so he thought he could sail through. Sahil looked over his exam and gave him one more final project. If he emailed it to him by the end of the week, and if it met his approval, he could take the next class. This was his last chance. Getting into the university was the first hurdle; keeping up was another beast. If this kid did not prove himself, he was done.

Finally, after hurriedly shoving last-minute toiletries and gifts into his suitcase, he jumped into the cab and headed to the airport. It never got old, this nervous tension when he went through airport security. As a Muslim male, he was often flagged for a search. He kept his head down and his voice respectful. He knew he had nothing to worry about. But this was post-9/11 America. Even after fourteen years, he carried the shrapnel of that destructive narrative on him, like a scarlet letter.

Finally, he was seated on the plane. The humming of the jet engine began to lull him into a mild stupor. As he placed his headphones on, the slow realization dawned on him that it had been over a year since he had gone back home to Pakistan.

Thank goodness for email, Zoom chats, WhatsApp, and Facebook, which helped him stay connected to everyone. Although he had to admit, sometimes there was an avalanche of excessive information online. Too many chat groups, and he really didn't need to know every third cousin who was getting married, engaged, or having a baby. Travelogues of distant relatives and every intake of food that some of his friends were eating were getting under his skin. He just wanted to see how his younger sister Annie's exams were going and that Ammi was doing all right since his father, or "abba," passed away two years ago.

He was glad to see that his mother was keeping herself busy with the charity work that was so dear to her heart. The Thalassemia Society had always gotten a lot of support from his family since one of his sisters passed away from the disorder when she was just eighteen months old. The fatal blood disorder was something none of them knew or had heard about before. Some said it was because his parents were second cousins, but over the last ten years since they began the organization, they had met many groups that had patients from all over the world who were not related at all. The disorder was usually not even detectable until the child was over ten months old because the baby lived off the mother's healthy hemoglobin cells until then. At that stage, the bone marrow of the child could not produce its own hemoglobin (or healthy blood cells), and the anemia set in. The monthly blood transfusions would keep the blood cells in the body to sustain a normal hemoglobin level.

By the time his baby sister was diagnosed, it was too late. Her small pale body could not take the transfusions because she had an allergic reaction to the blood that was given to her. They tried to get a match for a bone marrow transplant, but the blood banks that processed the pints of blood from donors could not find any match—at least not in time. The most tragic part of this for Sahil was that he was not a match, and neither were his sisters or other family members. The baby had a rare blood type, and everything they tried had failed.

His mother had been heartbroken. Seeing her despair, the only way out was to help others navigate the system so that they would not have to suffer such a great loss. The irony of it all was that the patients who were in the greatest need for medical care had the most dire of circumstances. They were villagers or labor workers, many with just one son to help with the lands or business. His health-care costs would be phenomenal, and then inevitably, his death would be the end of their livelihood. Then there was the daughter that was brilliant and had gotten accepted into a good school but had to drop out because the hospital visits were creating too many absences. Plus, there was the cost of the transfusions or medicine, which were equal to a month's wages or more. The hospital and clinic provided free medical care to those patients who simply would have been destitute without it. This cause had become a part of his family, and everyone played their parts in it one way or another. The summers he spent volunteering at the clinic were the most rewarding and heartbreaking. Life is so fragile, and there were so many factors—from luck to genetics—that could work in one's favor or not. He had thought of going into medicine for that reason, but since two of his sisters pursued the profession already, he was able to go into engineering, his first love.

Sahil's eyelids were getting heavy now, and he let the much-needed sleep take over his body as the plane took its course over the oceans and toward the other side of the world.

The sector of Islamabad where Sahil's family resided was a sleepy little part of town with an enclave of whitewashed homes set against the lush green mountains. There was a large international community established here, made up of a cosmopolitan potpourri of diplomats and established government officials. Elegant evenings of garden parties with beautiful women, witty men, and white-gloved "bearers" were commonplace among the social set.

Then there was the old city of Rawalpindi, which juxtaposed and contrasted so visibly that one had to take a second look back when passing through from one part of the city to the other. The makeshift tents and tattered clothing of mangy-looking children yearning for some food or money was a sight that always broke Sahil's heart, although he knew that many of these beggars were part of a well-established system. He was well aware of the paradox that this represented. The empathy he felt for these impoverished souls was something he had always felt inside himself. It would be easy to become immune to the poverty and look away, but that was, thankfully, a choice he never had to make. Each person had that responsibility, within their own reach, to help out. Each person can make a difference. This he knew for sure. He ignored his mother and sisters when they tried to stop him from giving money to the beggars, even if it meant they would just be handing it over to their boss. This didn't matter to him; they would have something to show at least. Other times, he would be getting something to eat at a café or a kebab house, and he would see them gathering outside, waiting for a handout. He would purchase several plates of kebabs with rice or fresh naans and invite them inside to sit at the booths or tables, their big gangly smiles spreading as they clamored in. The café owners or shopkeepers always scolded him for this, but it was such a small act, and for one day, these kids could feel some happiness. That's all it really was.

In an ideal world, the government and leaders of a country would subsidize such care for their people. Unfortunately, the corruption and greed had infiltrated the mindset of government workers and businessmen alike, seeping in like a virus. Those with any control were corrupted by a system that entitled even the smallest transaction for a percentage of the pot so they could line their pockets with the millions that came from foreign governments or in aid packets. Inevitably, it was the NGOs and private sectors that were picking up the slack. It all started at the top, and then others would follow suit. So if the leaders were corrupt, the rest became accustomed to the taste of black money—so much so that any objection to this became the crime itself.

Islamabad

There is an immediate and visceral punch to the senses when one disembarks on the tarmac in Islamabad. For Sahil, it is home, both familiar and distant—an anomaly that was, of late, becoming more and more apparent to him. The smell of diesel jet fuel, the hot tar of the runway, and the warm tropical scent of green foliage wafting from the palm trees and grass. Then there was smell of humanity, like fruit that had ripened beyond its use, pungent yet sweet. One could smell and feel the toil and earth of the people here; there was no getting away from it. Being away for so long, he was no longer unaware of this. Western airports were vacuous and sterile, encased in their glass domes, and each area was marked with perfect fonts and bold signs. The lighting was bright and the windows shiny and clean. One could definitely get used to that sense of order, he supposed, but right now, he happily breathed in the warm nostalgic atmosphere with all the dust, heat, and drudgery that it was.

After collecting his bags, Sahil proceeded out to the exit of the main airport, where a throng of anxious eyes were waiting for their own people to come out.

"There he is! I see him!"

He immediately recognized Annie's voice, and he waved to her as she was shouting and jumping up and down. Her chestnut-brown hair was partially covered with a long white scarf (or dupatta), and she wore a simple cotton kurta and jeans. His mother was in her traditional *shalwar* suit and always looked like she was ready to go to a tea party. How he admired that about her. No matter what life threw her way, she dressed up every day and put on her nice jewelry and had a smile on her face. Her elegant features still captured the beauty that she was. Tears were welling up in her eyes as she hugged him tightly. "Oh, *jaan*, how I have missed you!"

"Missed you too, Ammi," Sahil murmured into her cashmere shawl, the scent of her Chanel No. 5 achingly familiar and comforting as she held him tight. He was almost a foot taller than her, but her five-foot five-inch frame was tall for a Pakistani woman.

Sahil looked at his sister quizzically and smiled as she hugged him. Standing next to her, waiting patiently, was Maula Baksh, their driver. "Salaams, Sahil Baba." He saluted as he put the bags in the trunk.

"Oh Hoh, salaam. Salaam, MB!" Sahil replied cheerfully, giving him a hug. Maula Baksh had been with the family since Sahil was a young kid, and he was more like a distant uncle. But the old man always kept his demeanor formal in public and for the lady of the house, Sahil's mother, who treated him like an elder brother. This kindly old fellow had been there through all the difficult and happy times that Sahil's family had endured and celebrated over the years.

As they piled into the car and were seated, Sahil turned toward Annie. "What is this dopatta-on-the-head business?" he asked her, referring to the scarf as she clutched his arm.

"Oh, it's silly. But nowadays, there are all these Talibani-type beardoes roaming around. They are just so creepy looking, and I don't want to give them an opportunity to make their stupid comments."

"What comments?" Sahil asked, astonished and confused because this was Islamabad, not Peshawar. Any extreme type of behavior was always looked down upon here, especially with so many foreigners and diplomats around.

His mother piped in, "Beta, things are not the same here. These extremists are everywhere, and kidnappings and assaults are becoming commonplace, especially when they see young girls in Western clothes. I told her to get a bigger shawl, but we were running late." She glared at her daughter, who rolled her eyes and turned back to her brother.

He felt a combination of rage and fear overcome him for the fact that his family—his sisters and mother—needed to endure this when he could not be here. They had many close family and friends nearby, but if anything were to happen to them, he would feel responsible and devastated. They were all he had in this world.

He clutched his sister's arm tighter and pulled her hair gently. "So, monkey, heard your exams went well. Did you fill out your university applications yet?"

Her large almond eyes and fair complexion likened her to Audrey Hepburn, so much so that her friends nicknamed her Addie. She had even thought of cutting her hair short but changed her mind when she realized that her long hair made her look more mature and fashionable. "Oh, definitely. I need you to look over the essay for Yale, but the others are done. I am so hoping I get into Wellesley so I can be near you!" she bubbled excitedly.

"That is not a good enough reason to want to go to a certain college, Annie. You will have to decide on a major and then see which is best suited to you. Besides, I am only there for another year, inshallah."

She grimaced but then broke into a huge smile. "Okay, Dadajan. Whatever you say!"

Sahil just looked at her with wide eyes and laughed wholeheartedly. It was good to be home.

The car pulled up to the circular driveway, where his other two sisters and aunt were standing under the pergola. How he missed the heady scents of the *Plumeria* trees and lush jasmine that bordered their garden and house. This was the house he grew up in, where his father used to come home from work every evening with some treat or another for them. Sahil caught a tightness in his throat when he thought about this, the smell of warm sweet jalebis or samosas wrapped in brown paper would still be in his father's hands when he scooped Sahil up in his lap. His eyes were smiling and so warm.

"Salaams, Khala, Hana, Sofy. Wow, everyone looks so festive and great. I missed you!"

This was met with hugs and tears amid a flurry of crème silk and cotton scarves and embroidered long kurtas dotted with jewel colors as they ushered him into the main living room. "Of course, we had to dress up for the VIP arrival of our prodigal son!"

His mother asked the driver to bring in his bags, but he refused to let the old man carry such heavy suitcases up the front steps. "Ammi, really, I can do this. The poor guy looks like he is on his last legs. It's enough that he is still driving!" He whispered this to his mother, who agreed with him. But the default mode here was always that servants were there to take care of everything that the householders really don't want to do. A bitter remnant from colonial times, which left a bad taste in his mouth.

Hana and Sofy were older than him by several years, and he had always looked up to them. Annie was the baby, and since she was only a few years younger than him, their relationship was more like best friends. He had brought small gifts for all of them, and as he opened his bags to get them out, he heard a car pull up outside and come to a screeching halt.

"Sahil, you SOB! Why didn't you tell us you were coming a day early!" His friend from childhood, Mukhs, stormed in the room and jumped on him, giving him a huge bear hug.

This led to some friendly punches and laughter while the women looked on.

"Mukhtair, *janu*, you know that I needed him to myself for at least a day before you boys start taking him out, then the trip to Swat, and before you know, it is time for him to go back."

A broad grin exploded on Mukhs's face. "Okay, Khala. I get it. But man, it's good to see you, Sahil," he said as he slapped his friend's hand in a high five.

Mukhs was more like the brother that he never had. He finished his MBA at Georgetown last year and then took over his father's construction and management business, mostly building homes and selling them or renting out to the embassies or NGOs in Islamabad and Karachi. They shared everything, including the heartbreaking loss of their fathers within a year of each other.

"I hope you are ready to do some serious mountain climbing in Swat, boss!" Mukhs went on. "I told everyone you are coming, so we have a big group going up with us."

"That sounds great, Mukhs. I can't wait. But if it's okay with you, I need to take a shower and eat something. The airplane food was awful."

He couldn't remember when he ate last since his schedule had been so hectic, and then he had to pack and leave for the airport. Kim wanted to take him out for dinner and drop him at the airport, but he told her he had already arranged a ride. That was not entirely true. He did call a taxi, but he didn't want to add to the already overeager expressions she was beginning to display.

But now the fragrant smells of the *aloo gosht* (goat curry with potatoes) and rice coming from the kitchen reminded him of how hungry he was.

"And, Mukhs, you are staying for lunch too," his mother stated. It was not a question, and they all knew the answer since he practically lived at the house when Sahil came home. "*Jaldi, jaldi,*" his mother quipped to the servants Laal-khan and Amir Bi to take the suitcases to the bedroom and start cooking the chapatis (the warm puffy flatbreads) for the afternoon meal.

Sahil gave her a look of disapproval, which she conveniently ignored. "Beta, are you going to go in the kitchen now and cook the chapatis for us? Has America changed you that much?" She laughed and gave him a tight hug. "It's so good to have you home, *mere jaan*."

Zaina

KARACHI (2015)

The empire neckline on the lilac-colored Chantilly lace *kameez* was cut to enhance her long neck and collarbones. At twenty-one, she was a beauty still waiting to come into her own. She wanted to wear the tanzanite earrings that her mother had made for her from the stones that Mamu had brought from Tanzania last year. She had designed them herself, and when her cousins saw the drawing, they too wanted such earrings, so four sets were made. They were encased in an intricate gold mesh pattern and had fine chains holding the large purplish-blue emerald-cut gems that dropped just below her earlobes.

Having lived all her life in America, Zaina found that she was drawn more to Western-style fabrics and jewelry than the traditional ethnic garb that her mother and aunts wanted her to wear. Fortunately, she knew how she could merge the styles and get the simplified version—a fusion of East and West, in a way. The long scarf in the matching lilac silk was draped to one side and contrasted well with her thick ebony locks, brushed and blow-dried to a shiny wave. It was fun going to the salon here because she didn't have to explain anything about what look she wanted or how to manage her hair. The stylists had all the latest magazines and knew what fashionable looks the girls were wearing now. They always asked what kind of outfit you were wearing: pants suit, shalwar kameez, sari, or something different. Somehow, they knew exactly which hairstyle would suit what outfit according to the girl's face cut and texture of her hair. Besides that, the cost was the same as a cup of Starbucks in the US. Sometimes Zaina would feel bad and give double the tips, which her cousins frowned upon, saying that she was spoiling it for them. So she had to do this very discreetly.

As she came down the staircase into the foyer, she first wanted to peek into her grandmother's room on the main floor and get her opinion before going out to the party outside. There was already a large crowd gathering outdoors, the guests sitting on the lawn chairs amid sounds of laughter and conversations. Nani Amma's room was a quiet and peaceful chamber, and the stately matriarch did not move from there during an event or on special occasions. The guests were required to come and pay their respects to her in her room. A serving trolley with the various dishes that the chef (or *khansama*) had prepared were brought there for her. She did not always eat everything, but she did like to taste the dishes, so as to make certain that each was properly prepared. She made a note of everything, and there was a "postmortem" meeting the next day to correct any errors.

This was Zaina's maternal grandmother. The house belonged to her *mamu*, or maternal uncle. It was the place where everyone gathered for all the major events in the family, and where they stayed all summer when in Karachi. To call it a house would be a slight understatement. This palatial white two-storied Mediterranean villa had filigreed terraces jutting from tall windows overlooking elegant Mughal-style gardens, which was maintained in immaculate perfection by a team of groundskeepers and household staff. Somehow though, Zaina never felt overwhelmed by the size and amount of activity here. It really surged with a positive energy and much love that her uncle and family filled it with.

Her grandmother was known as Shahbano Begum, descended from a long line of strong women, each making their way in their husband's worlds. For short, she was called Bano Begum or BB. Her name translated from Persian to "Lady King" (which, for that time, was a higher rank than just a queen). Somehow, her father chose the name that so aptly suited this regal matriarch as she ruled the household with a firm hand.

"Adabs, BB, aap kaysee hain?" ("Greetings, Grandmother. How are you?) Zaina always asked in Urdu even though her grandmother understood English. She wanted to practice her Urdu.

Zaina had started calling her BB since she was a young teen, partly to tease her but mostly because she could tell that her grandmother was amused by it. BB was the ultimate scholar of the Urdu language. She not only taught Urdu and Persian, but she was also a renowned poet and had authored several books of poetry. Her environment reflected this strong but poetic style. The room was large and light-filled, the moonlight streaming in from the tall French windows onto the facing and left wall, which overlooked the front garden. There was a Persian silk carpet on the polished marble floor in shades of deep sapphire and turquoise, and the windows were draped in a pale blue damask.

Zaina gently approached the elegant woman, who was draped in a gossamer-like white French chiffon sari. She was seated on a divan covered in crisp white cotton with two sapphire-blue satin bolsters on each side. Placed next to her grandmother was a silver-filigreed treasure chest-like object: the *paan daan*, a container for her betel leaves and all the accoutrements that were used to spread, fold, and serve them to guests as well as for herself. Her thin frame looked old but healthy as she was disciplined in her diet and prayed five times a day. One tall glass of chilled and salted lassi (or buttermilk) was her routine every morning. She would then enjoy a heavy lunch and another glass of lassi at night, sometimes in place of dinner. She enjoyed fresh juices and fruits in season and the occasional dessert. As the matriarch of the family, she did not take her position lightly, and a single look or comment from her to whomever she was conversing with could tip the scale from approval to sheer terror. The simple pair of gold bangles glistened on her paper-white wrists when she moved to adjust her glasses as she looked up at her granddaughter. She only wore one large ruby-and-diamond earring on her right ear.

Once, Zaina had asked her mother about this, and she was told never to broach her grandmother on this subject. The story goes that when Nani Amma was getting ready one morning, she put on one earring and then went looking for her favorite son, Khalil, to help her with the other one. She had named him after her beloved father, who had taught her everything that she knew to survive in this cruel world. Her grandmother had left that one lonely earring on all these years to remind herself of this lost son, and understandably, no one ever questioned this gesture. Nor did she speak of it. She hadn't realized that he had already gone out, and she called after him several times. Shortly thereafter, she received a call that he had been in a fatal car crash. He was only twenty-eight, engaged, and was just ready to start his life. To say that she was devastated by this tragedy would be unfair. She did not eat for days and would not speak to anyone for months. He was her favorite and the most handsome of her sons. To her nani, boys were the ultimate blessing, and they ranked in favoritism by their looks.

Zaina thought, from his pictures, that he looked like Cary Grant. He was about three inches above six feet with a strong frame and a movie-star face. Her grandmother left the earring on to remind herself of this lost son, and understandably, no one ever questioned this gesture in addition to the fact that she never spoke of it.

She looked up and smiled with pleasure when she saw Zaina standing in the doorway. "Ahh, mere hoor, idar aou." ("Come here, my angel.")

Zaina came closer and bowed as her grandmother gently touched the top of her head, an automatic gesture of blessings that radiated a positive energy that Zaina embraced every time. The faint smell of sandalwood and rosewater drifted into Zaina's senses.

BB gleamed in her approval. "How lovely you are looking, my darling. Such English style!" She announced this with a strong punch at the end and a half smile. That was what Zaina loved so much about this woman. She was highly intuitive and always spoke her mind. That could be a lethal combination, but of course, at eighty-six, she had earned the right to speak freely on any matter. Zaina had a feeling though that she carried this trait from birth, and age had nothing to do with it. As far back as she could remember, this was what her grandmother represented—the truth in all its glory and sham. There was a certain confidence in the truth, that authentic knowledge that clears the air and puts all the cards on the table. This quiet room of sandalwood and silk was where she could always count on it. She would ask her one day about the earring, but only when the time was right. Surely, she would have a beautiful story to tell, and Zaina would relish it.

She did not take the last part of the elder woman's comments to heart, though she knew the value of staying true to one's heritage and rituals in every way was a priority in this household. On the other hand, much to Zaina's annoyance, her grandmothers' generation came from a school of thought that put a high price on lighter skin. She knew this was a form of racism and traced back to the era of colonialism that had permeated through previous generations and was still very much prevalent today.

The fact that she made no excuses for favoritism according to this was one of the layers that Zaina had accepted in her grandmother, among many other qualities that made her a very complex person. Even though Zaina's golden wheat coloring was not to match the very fair skin tone of her sister or cousins, her grandmother, as if exercising a regal amendment, made her the exception. Zaina knew that they had a special connection through poetry, long talks late into the night translating Ghalib or Mir, laughing over a cup of afternoon tea as she learned of the antics of various family members and the hardships of that life long ago when she migrated from India after the Partition. Zaina was curious of that era and life of which she knew nothing about and opted to spend time with her grandmother over other activities to learn more. So much so that her cousins had to drag her out with them on many occasions, complaining that she was turning into a senior citizen. Her time in Karachi was so limited that somehow, she understood that being young and having fun were not as urgent as the precious hours that her grandmother had to bestow upon her in her twilight years.

Besides, for all the emphasis on skin color, she knew that BB was not as superficial as she let on. The tone was not for disapproval but more to state a fact. The elder woman's sharp eyes did not miss the understated elegance of her granddaughter's attire, contrasting to all the other cousins' choices of traditional heavy silks in rich colors and heavy jewelry. She did not need to comment on it. They had an almost telepathic way of communicating, and each knew what the other was thinking.

Zaina tipped her head to one side, smiling, and performed a mock curtsy. There was a crack in that stern veneer as Bano Begum motioned to her granddaughter to leave the room. Suppressing a smile, she told her to go enjoy the party and to be sure to report back anything interesting.

As she went out onto the veranda and into the garden, Zaina looked for her cousins and her mother. She was unaware that she was getting admiring stares from several guests with the soft lilac color setting off her amber-brown eyes and copper skin tone.

The garden had been transformed in a matter of hours. Fairy lights were spun on the trees, and a row of tables with crisp white tablecloths were lining the far-left hedge. On top of these were large copper and silver chafing dishes, urns steaming with several types of saffron-soaked biryanis, almond-infused kormas, and vegetable dishes. Colorful salads were decorated on large silver platters, and lanterns were lit on each corner of the boundary walls. One corner was decorated for the desserts and tea with a cascading floral arrangement of bougainvillea and jasmine. Everyone seemed to be in a festive mood.

As she approached her uncle to compliment him on the arrangements, she noticed a very familiar face in a beautiful pink silk sari staring at her from the other side of the garden.

The young woman came darting over. "Zaina, is that you?" she said incredulously, flinging her perfectly straightened waist-length locks over her shoulder and wrapping her arms around Zaina. "Look at you rocking that Chantilly lace. You look stunning!"

Zaina was suddenly taken aback. "Oh my god. Shae, I can't believe you are here. This is my uncle's house. I am staying here for the summer. What are *you* doing here?"

Her uncle turned toward both of them and roared in a loud laugh, "You girls catch up. I am going to see what is keeping your aunt. And, Shahana dear, tell that fiancé of yours that I will be speaking to him later."

The girls laughed and looked questioningly at each other. "This is an incredible coincidence! I was invited because my fiancé is working with your mamu, and he invited me to join him tonight. I am staying at our Karachi house just down the street!"

Zaina was surprised not only to see this very modern girl in a traditional sari but that she was engaged. She was drop-dead gorgeous in a very old money sort of way. Her clothes and shoes were always the latest styles from London and Paris. Her schedule revolved around her weekly hair and mani-pedi appointments, and their family travel was set by seasonal shopping and fashion weeks in Paris and Milan. She had been invited to go to the seasonal showings at Paris Fashion Week once with Shae and her mother, but Zaina couldn't manage the funds or the time to do so.

Shae's family lived in a stately courtyard home with an indoor and outdoor pool. Her father had been a senior member of the UN as well as having served as the economic advisor to the previous prime minister. He passed away several years ago, so it was just Shae and her mother now. She and Zaina ended up exchanging numbers, and Shahana would always call her to talk or just hang out. She was famous for her lavish parties—the few that her mother did allow her to attend. Suffice it to say, her boyfriends were as varied as her shoe collection. She always seemed like the type of girl that would end up with an Arab sheikh or a European financier.

The fact was that Zaina enjoyed this wild child's unconventional attitude toward life. It was a nice break from all the typical traditional restrictions and her boring existence that she was forced to adhere to at home. Shahana introduced Zaina to designer clothes, the art of finding the right hairstylist, and rock music. She even took Zaina to her first rock concert.

Though she had a gaggle of posh friends, Zaina knew that they became close because Shae could count on her authentic opinions and cut through any of the bullshit that people dished out to her to get into her circle. Zaina was sort of an outsider in that ultrarich group. Her family was strictly middle class, with values on education and a more conservative outlook. Zaina understood that, at the end of the day, money did not make a better person, nor did it determine a good friendship. She had seen many families that showed off their extreme wealth for years, only to later become bankrupt, their homes foreclosed due to illegal activity or bad management. Some of the kids of these families got into drugs or dropped out of college as they had access to an unlimited allowance as well as parents who left their kids on autopilot from a young age.

Shahana was different. She never showed off or talked about money. In fact, she saw through all that, and they could just be themselves and laugh at the world together. It wasn't until late in her college years that she understood the difference of having enough money to live well and being extremely wealthy. Shae and her family were wealthy; they never had to worry about money. But they were also rooted in strong family ties and were generally happy people. They knew how to enjoy life and used their wealth to do so, as well as support a lot of good causes.

They say that the difference between a happy and unhappy life is gratitude—appreciating whatever you have. It's also the confidence to know that all this is just temporary. She realized early on that a good friendship was the difference between looking good and feeling good. A good friend makes you feel good; superficial friends make you look good. Her friend was one of those very special people that had the money but was unaffected by it. "It's just a fact of fate, lucky me!" She always said this with absolute sincerity, and Zaina loved her for it.

"Wait, wait. Back up here, Shae. You are *engaged*? When, where, and to whom may I ask? How come you never said anything when we met before I was leaving?" Zaina implored her with wide eyes.

"I know. Isn't it all so crazy? I had no idea then. I came here for a holiday, and Mum introduced me to this guy. I wasn't even in that frame of mind at all. Believe me, Zaina." Her excitement at telling the story of their "meet-cute" was palpable. "Apparently, his family owns half of Karachi, bankers and all. They happen to be family friends, and we went out for coffee a few times. And then…" She winked with an adorable smile that set her dimples even deeper. "A little more than coffee!"

Zaina burst out in a huge smile. "Of course, Shae. I would not have expected any less from you!"

"Hey, I always test drive before I buy a car, don't I? So why should a future prospect, ahem, for the rest of my life be any different!" She rolled her heavily mascaraed eyes in an as-if look and continued, "I told him that there is no way that I could live in Karachi after growing up in America, and he just laughed. Can you believe that? He just laughed! When I asked him what was so funny, he said that I could live like a queen in Pakistan or a worker bee in America. My choice. Though they have homes in New York, London, and the south of France. I asked him why he thought I would be a worker bee, and what does that mean anyway? He said that in America, you have to do everything yourself. And if I wanted to work, that's great. But everything is much harder there. Here it's all taken care of, and I could decide where we would want to live anyway. He said that it was love at first sight for him! Well, that was a hard argument to win, and things just moved forward from there, see. Voila!" She put out her left hand and displayed a huge cushion-cut diamond ring surrounded by a row of tiny yellow canary diamonds flashing on her finger. It was gorgeous and suited her long manicured hand.

"Wow, this is fantastic. How beautiful! I am so happy for you." She paused, still a bit thrown off and confused by the sudden announcement. "But hey. What about Khalid, Isham, or Lucca?" Zaina questioned, remembering the Saudi prince, the Lebanese entrepreneur, and her latest, the adorable Italian model she had been dating just a few months ago.

"Shush! You are going to get me into trouble, woman!" her friend scolded her as she pulled Zaina off to one side of the garden. "That was all silly fun, love. You know that when it comes to marriage, you have to see the whole picture and financial security. It even turns out that we have a lot in common as well as friends we both know. And hey, all this gorgeousness"—she mimics a model pouting and flailing her arms up and down from head to toe—"doesn't come for free, baby!"

They both laughed, and Zaina gave her friend a tight hug.

"Besides," she added, "Haroon is a dish. We hit it off right away. Come on. I have to introduce you!"

She clutched Zaina's hand and led her to the other side of the party where a tall, broad-shouldered, and handsome young man was standing. He wore a navy linen blazer and pants and a pale yellow Brooks Brothers-type pin-striped shirt with gold and lapis cufflinks.

"Haroon, you won't believe this, but Muzaffar Uncle is Zaina's *mamu*. She is staying here with them for the summer, and we know each other from America!"

He turned his gaze to her with bright and cheerful eyes, and his dimpled cheeks gave way to a friendly smile. Zaina liked him immediately.

"Well, what a small world," he said. "Salaams, Zaina. It's a pleasure to meet you." He spoke with a clipped British accent and bowed his head as Shahana came and stood next to him, looking as if she had known him all her life. "Then you must come for the engagement party next week. We would be honored to have you."

"Of course, I would love to. Thank you! It's such a pleasure to meet you, Haroon. And…you should know that Shae is one of my best friends, so I hope you know how lucky you are! One thing for sure, you will never be bored!" She smiled and exchanged a look with her friend that transported them back to times shared and secrets cherished.

"That, my dear, is an understatement. Luck has very little to do with it. I had to offer her the world to convince your friend to marry me against all odds, and I do consider myself very lucky that she accepted." He smiled broadly and looked over at Shae as they exchanged glances and, for what it was worth, some sparks for sure.

Zaina only hoped that her friend knew what she was getting into. Shae was such a smart girl. After all, she had completed her master's in finance from Wharton in less than the two-year program. Not to mention that she had that financial genius gene from her father. But when it came to matters of the heart, Zaina thought that people made the strangest choices.

That night, Zaina could not stop thinking about the fact that her very modern friend from America made a very snap decision to follow such a traditional path for the rest of her life. How did one know? Was it solely based on financial reasons, like a business deal? Was it about being in the right place at the right time and then following your instincts? Had she missed an opportunity because she wasn't thinking that way? Who knows? This was all too complicated and not something that she would have to worry about for at least another two years. She had completed her undergraduate degree but definitely was planning to do her masters or at least work for a couple of years. This trip should give her some breathing room to make those decisions.

The gallery downtown seemed very interested in hiring her and even suggested that they would help with her masters in curative arts if she was interested. She felt very fortunate to have such an opportunity. As she reassured herself, her mother's voice kept echoing in her mind when she told her about Shae. *If Shahana can get engaged so quickly, then you shouldn't be so indecisive either. So many interested families and you are behaving as if you have all the time in the world! Nobody will be waiting for you so many years while you decide on the right time. We should move quickly. Otherwise, all the good prospects will be gone!*

This need to push for marriage by her mother was part of the ongoing dispute and tension between them for the last few years. The traditional route of finishing up an undergraduate degree as a stepping stone to marriage had become antiquated in Zaina's mind, and she wanted to see and do so much more than that stage of life could offer her. She knew this was a common generational shift that was happening in their culture, but if she did not hold her own, she would be easily swept into that kind of mentality.

After the guests had left and the aftermath of the party was being sorted and put away, Zaina wandered into her grandmother's room to find her still awake and reading the newspaper on her divan. She looked up when she saw her granddaughter's sullen expression, and a shadow of concern crossed her face.

"What happened to you, *mere hoor*? Did you not enjoy the party?" She patted the empty place next to her on the divan. "Come. Sit with me for a while."

"Oh no. It's not that, Nannima," she replied. "The party was lovely, of course. I am just a bit tired, I think."

Her grandmother motioned for her to come and lie down and placed Zaina's head on her lap as she stroked her hair gently. "It is a good thing you did not get kidnapped by any of those nosy women looking for wives for their snooty sons. You are too naive for that crowd," she quipped.

Zaina popped her head up and looked quizzically at her grandmother. "How did you know they were looking? Did Mummy tell you about Shahana?" Zaina then went on to explain her confused state and how anyone can make such life-changing decisions in a matter of weeks.

Her grandmother simply listened and smiled. "God works in mysterious ways, my love. And for every person, there is a fate and a match that has greater meaning than we will ever know. You are wiser than you think, and you will know. And even if you don't, you must follow your instincts. Have faith that the stars, universe, and yes, our great God has a master plan for you." She paused. "Remember, my dear. You must find that partner that values you. He should be aligned with your dreams and talents. Otherwise, you will just be an adornment to his world.

"Our beloved prophet, peace be upon him, was an employee of Bibi Khatija. She was a businesswoman. And when she saw his honest way of dealing and doing business, she fell in love with him, and they married. She was forty, and he was twenty-five. Can you believe that? It was unheard of in those days! She found that genuine beauty of trust between them by God's grace. That is something our men never discuss or see as an example to honor their wives."

"But, BB, didn't Nana adore you? And didn't you love him?"

Her grandmother smiled faintly, and there was a distant look in her eyes that Zaina could not pinpoint. "I will tell you something, darling Zaina, that I have never told anyone else. Your *nana* was a great man, a nobleman whose proposal for me was for a second wife, to fulfill his needs. I was only sixteen, but I knew I had some talent, something inside me that needed to grow. My desires, talents, and need to write poetry was foreign to him and, in fact, a deterrent to his view of what his world was.

"Men are creatures of their own desires. When I could not—nay, would not—bend to his needs, he discarded me for another wife. This was not a world that I could tolerate, and I chose to leave him, with my children. It was just one year after the Partition, so we had family in Pakistan who housed us until we could make it on our own."

Zaina looked up at the elegant matriarch who ruled her son's home like a queen and wondered in disbelief that any man would not have valued her beauty and talent with pride. "But why did your parents marry you to such a man, BB? You must have had other choices."

"Ah, my dear. We lived in a different time then. My father wanted me to further my studies, but my mother—your great-grandmother—had other ideas. And the culture ensured that such a proposal from a great nawab like your Nana was valued much higher than any needs of a girl's desire to further herself. I was grateful for the fact that he gave me five beautiful children, but when I left him, it was a difficult life to start over. I never needed anyone else, and my writing gave me a purpose, more than any palatial home or servants could. I would have lived in a shack with someone who knew my life's purpose and valued my talents if that was my destiny. I was fortunate. God looked over me and us. If not for my own drive to further my writing and the support of those who valued it, I would not have been successful or been able to see my children grow into the wonderful human beings that they are, and…" She added this with a warm smile and an embrace as she held Zaina close, "Then I would not have you, my dear Zaina beta. Just promise me that you will not settle for just anyone who looks good on the surface. Beauty and wealth are those tricks that fade with time. The one that cherishes, values, and loves you for who you really are inside, in your soul—that is the partner in life that will fill you to the depths of the earth. You will understand when you find that person. I haven't lived this long to tell you that I have all the answers, only that you must ask the questions. Ask why. Why am I here, and what is my purpose? Ask why you must bend to another's will when you know there is another path that is better for you. It takes courage and faith to do this, my dear, but do it you must."

Zaina had so many more dilemmas spinning in her head. *Did her grandmother have another great love other than her writing? Was she destined to find such a unicorn who had all those traits?*

It was late now, and she needed to get her sleep, as did this amazing woman who happened to be her grandmother. "Thank you, BB, for sharing this with me. I am so touched and so grateful that you honored me with this history of your life and dreams and advice. I will cherish it always. I love you so much."

She had never seen this woman show much emotion, but now there were tears in her clouded gray eyes. She held her close and bid her good night. BB responded, in a voice that was clearly straining to hold back her emotions, with the familiar nightly greeting, "Shab bakhair, mere jaan." ("Fair night, my love.")

Upon returning to her room, Zaina changed into her cotton pajamas and crawled under the cool sheets. She tossed and turned several times before sleep finally overcame her. The anxiousness and her mother's disdain for her need to be independent slowly began to be diffused by her grandmother's gentle and loving wisdom. She was also looking forward to getting away to the mountains of Swat in a few days. Just the thought of being there eased her mind like a comforting coat of warm milk, and she slept without another thought.

The next morning, at breakfast, everyone was talking about the trip to Swat Valley. Her immediate family had been going there every summer for as long as she could remember.

Her father's eldest brother, her uncle who had reached spiritual enlightenment through the Sufi order, had built an estate there that was truly a paradise. People flocked from all over the world to meet him there and obtain spiritual guidance as well as just to spend time with him.

Zaina never quite grasped the weight of her uncle's importance in the spiritual world because he was so loving and kind, and she just loved to be in his presence and listen to his stories and even his jokes. But time did seem to come to a standstill there, as if one only had to soak in this life at this particular moment. She hesitated to discuss this with many people. It was too close to her heart and too deep to elaborate. And until a person actually was able to go there and experience it, there was nothing that could explain this state of mind.

Any description or explanation would fall short of the mystical quality that permeated this place.

This time, there was a large group of cousins going, so her mamu and father rented a large van and arranged for the flights to Islamabad. The younger ones would need a *doli* (or palanquin) because the five-mile hike from the small village of Pier Baba could get rough over mountain terrain, and there were some waterways scattered in between.

When the arrangements were finally decided and the reservations made, Zaina went up to her bedroom and started to pack. Her cousin came in and asked what she was taking for the trip.

"Well, first of all, you will need jeans and comfortable shoes, Bina."

"Oh, that's not a big deal. But what about the evening parties and such? I will have to go shopping."

"Bina, there are no such parties in the mountains, silly. Just keep some simple kurtas and cotton outfits."

"You are kidding, right? What are we supposed to do every night then, for two weeks? What if there are some cute boys? I will have to dress up some time, and what about the big dinners?"

Zaina just looked at her beautiful young cousin and shook her head. There was no possible way to explain the placid beauty of a place where it did not matter what you wore, what you ate, or who you met. Especially to a young girl from the bustling city whose calendar was filled with parties and shopping and the only dilemma in her life was whether she would be up to date on the latest fashion trends.

This actually might do her some good, Zaina thought. *To connect with nature and realize that there is a greater world out there.*

Shahbano

Uttar Pradesh, India (1929)

Chanda had watched her village grow in the last few years. She was the daughter of a tenant farmer. Her father had prospered tilling the land, growing the golden wheat and bright yellow *sarson* mustard fields. Her mother had died after the fifth child, her last sibling to survive.

Over the last year or so, there were many hot, labored afternoons when she had watched the nawab stop by, surveying his domain and lands. When he strolled by, his tall frame overshadowing her demure father, Baba would start bowing and showing his respect for his employer and master. She would stand at the entrance, leaning on the doorway to their newly constructed mud home as the men spoke and exchanged thoughts on the progress in the fields. She did notice that the nawab looked over at her a few times. She was not one to shy away, and her curiosity got the better of her at these rare moments.

Now that she was past the marriage age at eighteen, her father had given up any prospects for her finding a husband. Being of a darker complexion and that age, there was not much hope for her future, and so he started training her to help him, more so due to the fact that there were no sons to take over this task and responsibility. The eldest daughter of a parent with no sons becomes the designated son, taking care of her siblings, seeing that the home is cared for, and caring for her father as well, especially without a wife to take that role. Both father and daughter fell into that rhythm as a natural progression.

There were rumors that her mother had bedded with one of the indigenous men in the forest area—the Bheels, as they were called. This could possibly account for her deep walnut skin color since both her parents came from the north and were of a lighter complexion. Her father ignored such gossip since it did not amount to any good. He was a simple man, and he chose to live a simple life.

Chanda enjoyed the work in the fields. She was strong and able and picked up the management and science of farming this land and how to handle the farmhands well. The idea of abandoning this was only because the nawab had approached her father personally with a substantial increase in pay for her to help be a house manager at the *haveli* and maybe do some of the farmwork. Her father was hesitant, but they needed the extra income, and he knew the nawab took note of Chanda's capability. The nawab was twenty-five years older than her, but she did not look at age as a factor anymore. These were just numbers to her. She was well aware of her attraction to him; that was all. Anything else would be her wild imagination playing tricks on her.

She was hired to help and manage the house staff. She would assist his second wife with daily chores while the Nawab Saab tended to the business of the land managers and tenant farmers. He could be gone for days or weeks, she was told, leaving his young wife with the three small children, who were already proving to be a handful for their mother and two nannies.

The village lands were known for the china mines splattered in the soaring mountains spanning the four thousand acres in this regional town known as Khayldi. The four thousand acres and, subsequently, the village was presented as a gift to the nawab by the Raja Aeel. And in return, he was to keep the native and indigenous peoples of the area in check and gainfully employed. Three years had passed before the nawab took over the land and the small village that had only consisted of a mosque and a few thatched huts alongside the river.

His first task was to build the haveli and main house with its expansive front verandah, polished marble floors, and intricately carved teak doors. The massive rooms all opened into the main center courtyard, where there was a fountain and a floor of mosaic inlaid with tiles of lapis and onyx. The five pillars—

which were weight-bearing and held up each section of the villa—reminded one of the importance of the number 5 in Islam. The five pillars, praying five times in a day, and as a learned man, the nawab had read that the number 5 held a universal meaning of certain significance for the five fingers on a hand and the five senses. For all his adherence to his own religion, he had read much, and his mind was open to learning. There were still the gardens and orchards surrounding the structure that needed planting. These would be gradually grown in time with the seasons.

When the haveli was completed, it was with the primary intention to prepare for his wife and children moving from the town of Bastar to settle here. He had already arranged with the dewan of Bastar to transfer some of the duties that he was designated to another lower nawab. It was more of a ceremonial position that he had there, and he was looking forward to performing more productive tasks and taking greater responsibilities in the village of Khayldi.

Much to his dismay, his wife, Anjuman Begum, refused to leave the bustling town where her four children were settled in their schooling as she had made a comfortable life for herself in Bastar society. No number of jewels or bargaining could dissuade her to come with him. She had been born into a prominent family herself and had acquired a strong sense of identity over the years in running his household here in Bastar. He valued her opinion, but at the same time, he had to maintain his own position as head of the household and a nawab in his own right. It was a fine balance, but now the scales were shifting.

It was when he realized that his plan to move her and the children to the village with him was futile that he decided to take a second wife. This was not an easy decision as he was not a man to create more confusion in his life. He sought solutions through hard work and discipline, and this was a solution-based decision—the only one that made sense to him and was not unusual for the times either. As a nawab of noble gentry, he was still considered young and good-looking. He was in his midforties and standing slightly over six feet, with light hazel eyes and skin like the color of a freshly peeled apple. He was still in his prime. His trimmed beard was scattered with just the slightest of silver streaks, and his presence commanded the attention of men and women alike.

As it happened, the search for a bride did not take long. Such news travels quickly in small towns, and before long, messengers were showing up regularly at the nawab's door. These were sent by the prospective families that were requesting an appointment to meet him.

The first wife, Anjuman Bai, by custom, would need to give her approval for this marriage. In fact, it turned out that she was gladly prepared to comply. She was completely done with having children after losing three babies and almost her own life in painful childbirth. The four children she had now (two sons and two daughters) were enough for her to secure her position and wealth for their future. Despite many years of longing and suffering, she had long lost the need for her husband's companionship or approval. His eyes had wandered more than once, and that sufficed enough to end the bond for her. Anjuman sent her handmaiden, Biban, to be present for the viewing and reviewing of prospective brides for the second wife position, and the woman reported back with details as instructed.

Most were very young, as was the norm. But too young, thought Anjuman, and they would have to wait to consummate the marriage. Too old and the woman would get quickly worn down after bearing the children (if she survived, that is). There would be little comforts, and an older or weaker wife would be no use in managing the household in that godforsaken village, she mused. This would mean he would again pressure her to join him or even take a third wife. The thought irked Anjuman to no avail.

There were several girls and families that seemed to be appropriately aligned to make a good match. One girl in particular caught her ear as she heard the family background and various details. She sent Biban to bring the girl to come see her with her mother. The fact that the father was a teacher was not lost on Anjuman. They would certainly appreciate their daughter going to a higher ranking in society as well as be assured of the monetary benefits for her to live a comfortable life.

Too many newly rich families sought quick fame and fortune through these types of alliances, and the families with royal blood had daughters with entitled attitudes but no skills to run a household on their own. Getting dressed by handmaidens and horseback riding would have no place in village life. Having been born into wealth herself, she had no patience for gold diggers. This blatant greed showed a lack of tact, and this she abhorred.

For all her wealth, she acknowledged that girls with good upbringing from good families were not greedy. They had education and solid bloodlines. And there was nothing wrong with parents wanting security for their daughters, but they were not desperate. They were God-fearing and had standards. That was what she placed in high esteem. "Hadee dhoondo" was what her mother always used to say. ("Look for the bones. That is where the family comes from.")

As a bonus, many of the prospects were not even close to the beauty that this Shahbano girl possessed. Her ebony locks were braided to one side under the light blue chiffon scarf, worn loosely on her head. She had a quiet nature but large bright eyes that showed her intelligence. She was well-read, a quality that the nawab could use in managing the village and burgeoning estate in that remote area. This one would keep him satisfied, and he would not pester her too often when he visited Bastar, she surmised.

* * * * *

Shahbano was the eldest of six girls and one brother. At sixteen, she had the porcelain complexion and willowy frame that all mothers wished for their daughters to possess in order to make good matches. Her father was a scholar and a teacher, and these traits he passed on to all his children. As a result, Shahbano absorbed this lifelong yearning for all things academic as if by osmosis. As a very young child, she would sit by her father's side, many times throughout the night, learning to read very quickly and begging him for stories about history and about the Prophet. And she was eager to memorize and recite poetry.

Khalil was not keen to see his favorite daughter married off so fast. He wanted to send her to Aligarh University, where they were finally accepting women. With her keen intellect and photographic memory, she would advance quickly, he was certain.

"Bibi," he said to his wife, "it seems that the nawab is almost my age." He continued to implore. "Shahbano is still very young. She can marry in a few years after she finishes university."

His wife turned and looked at him incredulously. "*Uff taubah.* Do you realize how lucky we are that the Nawab Saab sent his proposal for Shahbano? You have no idea how many families were trying to convince him with gifts of sweetmeats, silver goblets, jewels, and shawls. I simply brought the *halwa* I had made. In a silver tray of course, the one from my dowry. And she, Anjuman Bai Begum, seemed to take a liking to our Shahbano immediately.

"Besides, no husband wants a wife who is so educated that she becomes useless to keep up her household duties. You know that if she goes to university, she will be an old hag by the time she's done. No proposals will be coming then. Do you want her to remain a spinster? She is also the eldest. This will affect all the proposals for the rest of your daughters, who will be left stranded, waiting for Shahbano to get married, God forbid! You must stop putting these wild ideas in her head!"

Her voice was reaching a fever pitch by now, and her husband came over and patted her shoulder gently, nodding his head. "Yes, yes. I understand, my dear. But as a second wife, what rights will she have? I am sure we can wait for a suitable match for her as a first wife—an only wife. There need not be other wives in her life. We have seen all the politics and anguish that can cause in other families.

After all, you and I have lived as such and raised our family by the grace of Allah."

She looked at her husband, almost feeling sorry for his naivete and trust in a world that could be very cruel and harsh. She understood that being a second or even a third wife in a rich household could be bearable if your future was secure and your children had enough to prosper. He had no inkling of the hidden cupboards and ceramic jars she kept filled with rupees and coins that she had squirreled away over the years. This became extra income that his students' families offered on Eid or special occasions. She saved this income then and used it to procure any substantial needs for the family to compensate for his teacher's salary. She was hesitant to remind him of this, but her desperation to finalize the match overcame her female instincts to protect his sensitive nature and male ego.

"This is true, but God knows how we have struggled to make ends meet on your *munshi's* salary and my dowry. There will be another four years before our Qasim will finish his schooling and earn enough to allow your retirement. We will have to sell some land for the dowries of our daughters as well. The best part is that his first wife wants nothing to do with this arrangement. She is staying in Bastar because he will be moving to this village of his. Khayldi is much farther away and has four thousand acres with teak forests and china mines. He has already built the main haveli with marble floors and ordered carpets and furniture to be made. Isn't that wonderful? Our daughter will live like a queen! It is a blessing that this proposal came for Shahbano, my husband. You must believe me."

Khalil felt his arguments had been trumped by his wife's dearth of information on the nawab and prospective life for his beloved Shahbano. He finally acquiesced, recognizing his wife's practical nature and what seemed to be a keen vision for the future of his daughter and their family.

Shahbano listened to the conversation between her parents carefully. She knew that her comfortable life in her modest home was never going to be the same. She wanted to run over and hug her father, somehow helping him state her case. Such behavior was unheard of though, as her mother's word was stone and could not be moved. This she knew for sure. She could not muster the courage to be outspoken as this would be a sign of disrespect, and being respectful was, above all, the paramount objective in a good family. She quietly floated through the following days like a raft in a river, anticipating the rumbling and whirring of the waterfalls ahead.

Over the next month, her mother was in a flurry of packing her marriage trunk with her dowry and preparing for the wedding. The four silk saris, two hand-embroidered cashmere shawls, a small silver tea set, a carved wooden box with four bottles of attar perfume, and several silver items for her dresser were carefully wrapped in muslin cloths edged with silver filigree ribbon, which her mother had been sewing for many years in preparation for this day. Each layer was strewn with rose petals and dried jasmine buds.

In another crate for household items, there were copper cooking vessels and utensils, Chinese serving bowls, and silver trays. Mostly all of these had been handed down through the generations of past dowries and saved for many years. Her mother had also had two new bed quilts made with matching cushions. These were filled with pashmina wool and covered with an elaborate silk tapestry in woven threads of amber and gold. The wool was light but very warm. It was more expensive than cotton filling, but her mother had to maintain such a standard. The covers of the quilts were made from a sari from her own dowry. She had the nine yards cut into two pieces to create both quilts and cushions, matching up the design perfectly. It was a small sacrifice for her to achieve the final look, satisfied that this was what she had wanted to complete her daughter's dowry to the noble nawab.

There was also a small but elaborate Quran, gilded in turquoise borders and illuminated in gold calligraphy. It was handed down from her great-grandfather and had a mosaic silk cloth cover that it slid into like an envelope. This was her wedding gift from her father, and she knew how precious it was to him. She held it gingerly in her hands as she kept the tears from welling up in her eyes.

"Keep this safely, my dear Shahbano. Read it often, and may God always keep you in his protection."

The trunk was almost full when Shahbano quickly pulled several books of poetry and history from her father's shelves and rushed to slip them into the folds of the clothes at the bottom. She had a small folding writing table that she wanted to somehow also fit into the trunk, but it was not possible. As she sat on the floor next to the trunk, she felt an anxiety that she had never experienced before.

The writing table was certainly not a large item to take. Why was she trying to sneak it into the trunk? What instinct was she trying to stave off? she wondered. She would simply ask to take it with her in another box or crate.

Her mother quickly refused the request, saying it was a useless object and that she could always get another one. It was her father who realized the huge endeavor that his daughter was going to undertake, and he packed it carefully in another crate for her, ignoring his wife's' protests. He then went to the trunk and pulled out the books as she and her mother watched.

"These books will have their own place in Shahbano's new home, along with the writing desk."

He carefully wrapped them in papers and put them in the crate with the desk to take with the rest of the dowry. She knew this was a difficult move for her father to make, and she was ever grateful for it.

* * * * *

As the wedding festivities subsided and Shahbano's family parted ways, the *baraat* headed toward the nawab's family home by horse and carriage and on elephant. It took almost four hours as she shifted in her crimson and heavily gold-embroidered taffeta silk wedding dress. She was perched high on the bumpy and undulating elephant seat, and though it was a cool October evening, she could feel the beads of sweat forming on her neck and forehead from the heavy clothing and jewels. Her bangles jingled as she tried to peer out of the sheer pink curtains of the palanquin, but she could not recognize the landscape. She settled back in, resigning her fate to whatever would come.

Anjuman Bai was standing at the front of the doorstep, ready to welcome the new bride. Under normal circumstances, the first wife would not partake in this activity. But Anjuman was no ordinary first wife, nor was she a spring chicken with her bruised pride to show disdain to this new addition to her husbands' family. She had chosen Shahbano herself, and now she would hold her head up high and help the girl cross the threshold.

She began the welcome ritual by slowly pouring saffron-infused milk from a silver pitcher onto the new bride's feet as she entered her husband's domain. Shahbano did not know what to expect. Her mother never gave her any idea of these elaborate rituals, but she kept her head down and listened as each member of the family said some prayer and then fed her a sweet or touched her head. They sat her on a divan of deep blue velvet and gold and, in turns, held rupees that they circled around her head to ward off the evil eye and give alms to the poor.

Then the nawab came and sat next to her, his large frame dressed in the finest gold-threaded fabric for his sherwani that Shahbano had ever seen. From where she was sitting, she could only look at him partially, but the diamond-encrusted buttons and golden *saleem shai* slippers were beyond anything that her father or brother had ever worn. There was an aroma of jasmine flowers and rose attar in the air as he drew her henna-laced hand up and slid a large diamond-and-ruby ring on her delicate finger.

At that point, someone brought out a huge mirrored tray and placed it in her lap to perform the *arsi mursif* ceremony. She had seen this done many times at weddings but never understood the significance of it until today. It was the first time that the bride and groom would view each other, and the mirror was used to deflect the intensity of each other's gaze as they exchanged glances in the mirror.

Shahbano was glad of it—of not looking at him directly. His eyes were the color of honey, and he looked at her in a way that she did not know how to feel. He smiled and everyone laughed and cheered. She did not waver in her expression but just looked and then turned away. The moment was so awkward and intense that she just remained stoic until she was told what to do.

After all the revelry, they were ushered into one of the large rooms (his bedroom, she assumed). It was decorated with roses and jasmine garlands strewn about the large four-poster bed. She could hear voices at the door, and then the door shut. As she sat on the edge of the bed, he walked over and lifted her chin up so they were facing each other.

"You must be tired. It has been a long day. I will go wash up, and you can change too. Let's get some sleep, and we will talk more in the morning." With that, he began walking toward the door, and she realized he was leaving the room.

"Wait!" she called out, her voice even sounding foreign to herself as she had not spoken to anyone the whole day. "Nawab Saab," she addressed him carefully as she was instructed to do, "may I have my things sent to the room? I have some books and things that I will need."

He looked at her in a quizzical manner. "Oh, I didn't realize that you would be needing them today. I have already arranged for all your trunks and crates to be sent to Khayldi as we leave tomorrow. They will be there when we arrive. You have clothes and shoes in the *almari* as part of the *bardi*. You should find everything you need here."

And with that, he turned and left the room, closing the door behind him.

It was perplexing enough for her to be in this place with so many new faces, and she thought it even stranger that he just left her alone on their wedding night.

The next morning, Shahbano rose early, still not used to the silk pajamas and fancy new slippers. She longed for her weathered cotton sleeping suits and thin leather sandals. She did not sleep well. Though the bed was huge and soft, her mind was not at ease. How could her parents just let him send her things to that village? What if the books got wet or ruined on the way?

She dressed quickly. The chamois silk sari that was laid out for her was of a deep rose color, and a set of small rubies, entwined with diamonds, was sitting on the dressing table in a black velvet box.

She heard a knock, and an older woman entered, dressed in a cotton sari draped lightly over her head and carrying a tray with the morning tea and toast. "Salaams, Choti Dulhan Bai. I am Zainab. I am here to help you with anything that you need."

The woman came over and helped Shahbano put on the necklace and then twisted her hair into a bun as she adjusted the sari *palou* over her head. "You must wear the ruby tikka. You are a new bride, and it is the custom to dress with all your finery."

She then explained that these clothes were fine for the morning breakfast. But afterward, she would have to change into travel clothes for the journey to Khayldi, which could take up to two days, depending on the weather.

Shahbano peppered the woman with a lot of questions before they went to the huge dining room for breakfast, but Zainab was trained well to remain quiet and discreet. Shahbano would have to be patient to get all her questions answered.

She was not expecting a reception committee as she entered the room, but the table was set for twelve, and all the seats, save one, were occupied by family members, with the nawab seated at the head. He bowed his head when he saw her, but no other acknowledgment came from the others.

She quickly sat in the empty seat as she was served with the food on her plate. The first wife was absent from the table. There was a sense of cordiality in the air, but there was also something else. These family members were in the first wife's camp, and she could tell that they were not pleased with her presence.

"We will be leaving in an hour, Shahbano Begum, so please be ready." The nawab stood up and spoke in a matter-of-fact way. Then, without much fanfare, he left the room.

She had to blink and remind herself that she was now a *begum*, a wife of a nobleman. She already missed the old Shahbano and her family. The others also stood up and rumbled out of the room. Not without haste, Shahbano noted.

Zainab had already packed her wedding dress, jewels, and other clothes in a trunk that was being hefted onto a cart that would be accompanying the caravan to Khayldi. Except for the nawab, Zainab, and the drivers of the carriage and cart, there was no one else coming with them. The gaggle of relatives she had seen last night and this morning were nowhere to be seen, as if swallowed into the huge palatial walls of the nawab's villa here.

So very strange, she thought.

She climbed into the carriage with Zainab in tow as the nawab drove the other carriage himself.

It was a difficult journey, with jungles and rough roads meandering through various villages and forests. She was glad of the thick cotton trousers and jacket that had been given to her for the journey.

They stopped in the early evening before dusk and set up a campsite near one of the villages. The nawab was fond of hunting, and he went out with a few men from the area to shoot partridges or pigeons for the evening meal. Though they had packed dried fruits and foods, fresh game was always caught and preferred when available, Zainab explained.

A small fire and makeshift stove were set up as the driver and Zainab cooked lentils and rice. Shahbano sat on the cushions provided and wrapped the warm blanket around her as they enjoyed a hearty meal complete with grilled partridge. She noticed the nawab looking over at her at some point, the fire between them giving an amber glow to her face. He looked relaxed and quite handsome, she thought, though he was probably as old as her father. She shuddered at the thought, and at this, the nawab got up and said it was getting late. She should wrap up and plan to leave early in the morning.

When they finally reached the haveli in Khayldi, Shahbano was so exhausted, she was ready to just lie down on a flat surface anywhere. Her back was stiff, and it took all her effort to not stretch out as she exited the carriage.

Zainab had been here several times as she came to cook and help when the house was being built and set up. She showed Shahbano to her room to wash up and then began to unpack the trunks and crates. It was still early, so she wanted to help Zainab and make sure all her things had arrived in good condition.

As she was unpacking and putting away the things, the nawab came into the room. It was still unclear to Shahbano if they were to have their own rooms or she was to share this with him. He seemed very odd about this, and she did not have the wherewithal to make it clear. Though his language skills seemed quite sophisticated, personal communication did not seem to be his forte. Zainab, sensing her presence as a third wheel, got up and left the room.

"I hope you will find everything you need here," he said as he closed the door and walked toward her.

She stood up from the unpacking and looked at him directly. "Once my books are unpacked, I will feel more at home. If there is anything that is required of me, please let me know."

He was quiet for a moment and then abruptly pulled her onto the bed. She gasped and muttered a feeble cry as he unbuttoned his jodhpur pants, undoing her shirt and clothes as well. He held her tightly while consummating their marriage. When he was done, he pulled the quilt over her, and she lay there quietly, suppressing her muffled sobs until he left the room.

"We will have dinner in an hour. And tomorrow, I will show you the lands."

After that, Shahbano was keen to keep her distance from her husband and refused to accompany him to the farmlands, much to his dismay. *Is this how marriage and babies are formed?* The thought was incredulous to her. She would avoid him as much as possible. His behavior was so demeaning, and she felt shattered.

Her excuses over the many long months and eventual years were that she was either pregnant or in menses. This allowed her nine months of freedom from him and many days in the other months. Nevertheless, she had to perform her duties to him and to the household as instructed by her mother, and this was a task that she could not avoid, no matter how she tried.

It was these aberrations over the last several years that produced five children: three sons (Ashraf, Musharraf, and Khalil) and two daughters (Shahnaz and Zebunissa). It took her many years to realize that he was not a bad person. He treated her well otherwise, but his harsh and crude mannerisms and approach to physical intimacy caused her much anxiety. Because she did not know anything else and just assumed this was how children were born, her time with him was simply a duty or task that she had to endure.

She turned to her books and her poetry-writing, which allowed her to breathe life into her scars and escape from the harsh reality of this union. Her poems were sad, she knew, and some very heartbreaking. What else did she have to gather those thoughts and feelings together and make sense of this life?

She decided to send her work to a local newspaper that circulated in various towns. This could take months to reach, but at some point, the word was out that a female poet from a far-off village was showing much talent.

In the next few years, she began to gain a loyal following among other poets and lovers of the spoken word. This branched out to the outer towns and municipalities. Much to her husband's chagrin, she was invited to mushairas and poetry readings by fellow artists, which was not conventional for women to attend. She mustered up her courage and went in purdah—where her face was covered and men sat separately from the women—

so her husband could not object. And if for nothing else, she was stubborn for this.

She was dedicated to these two missions in her life. Her writing was for her survival, and her children gave her hope but needed constant attention. Unfortunately, the two miscarriages she had suffered through had weakened her, and she requested some help to be brought in. The nawab reluctantly agreed and ordered two nannies who helped take care of the younger baby and assist Shahbano when she taught the elder children herself. Her father had taught her well, and she knew how to educate children due to her experience with her younger siblings and cousins.

"I have hired another girl to help with the housework. Since you are too busy writing your poetry and in your books, she will manage the house. She is from a neighboring village and was recommended to me by one of the elders."

Shahbano did not know why, but he never gave such detailed explanations before for any decisions he made concerning the management of the home or lands. In fact, it was very common for him to hire and fire as he pleased, imposing his importance on a regular basis. Perhaps he felt guilty for admonishing her duties to a servant girl, she thought. He need not have worried about that though. There was no pride on her part, as far as that was concerned.

"Thank you, Nawab Saab. That is very kind of you. If that is not too much, I would greatly appreciate it. I will have more time to do the children's schooling as well as my writing."

She said this with sincere effort and could not imagine what may have provoked him to such sarcasm when he shot back at her. "Enough of your damn books and writing. If I wanted a scholar for a wife, I would have married the principal of the local school! Do you not understand what a nuisance you have become? Just stay out of my sight. I have more work and land than I can manage and do not need your flippant attitude!"

Shahbano's face became flushed, and she felt a tremor beginning to buzz inside her. How dare he speak to her that way, she thought. It took all her self-control not to throw something at his head, and she quickly turned around and fled the room.

The new girl arrived in a matter of days. Chanda came and, as planned, took over the kitchen immediately. Meals were suddenly very punctual, and beds and sheets were changed and washed more frequently. She may have been around eighteen or nineteen. She was younger than Shahbano only by a few years, but the wear and tear of a loveless marriage and childbearing had not tainted her youthful charm or figure. She was not beautiful or even lovely, but there was a fire within her that kept her energy burning bright, Shahbano noted with some disdain.

The large house was being maintained as it should have been, Shahbano supposed, but she did not care for such things now. She had time to write and spend with her children, whom she adored.

After a few weeks, when she was out in the garden with the children, she noticed that the nawab and Chanda were returning from the fields. They were laughing about something, and she wondered what that could have been. When was the last time she laughed with her husband? Was it a twinge of jealousy that she felt?

How can you be jealous of someone to whom you have no strong bond? she thought. Yes, he was the father of her children, but otherwise, there was no intimacy or connection between them. What did this Chanda have? And the true question was, why did she, Shahbano Begum, care at all?

The cart that they were on pulled up to the front of the house, and they climbed out. The girl was wearing a green printed cotton kurta and pajama sewn a few sizes too small. This Shahbano noticed as it revealed her lithe young frame.

"Salaam, Begum Sahiba. How are you this morning?" Chanda chirped and smiled while tipping her head toward Shahbano.

Ignoring her, Shahbano turned to her husband. "Nawab Saab, may I have a word with you? Chanda, you may go inside and tend to the kitchen." Her tone was stern, she realized, but not out of place.

The girl scurried off quickly, turning back once to look at the nawab.

He ignored the tone (or seemed to) and did not seem as tense and aggravated as usual as he smiled in her direction. "I hope the children are well? What is it you needed, Begum?"

"Is she tending to your farms as well now? I do not recall that that is what she was hired for."

"I am training her to understand the workings of the farming and tenant farmers so that when I am away, she can manage. She is very intelligent and has experience from her father, and mostly, she takes a great interest in all the work. I think she will do very well." He said this in an even tone, as if he was talking about any farmhand or a field-worker.

"I believe she has enough work to do with the house. You should find another worker to train for this task. Chanda will not be available."

He walked over to her and tightly wrapped one hand over her arm. His eyes glared with contempt. "You are not one to tell me how to run my lands, Begum. I will hire and fire as I please, and you have made it clear that you have no interest in such work. Your writing and books have greater importance to you than your husband and his work, so it's best that you stay out of it. And keep in mind that your needless meddling will not be tolerated!"

His voice had now become very loud and menacing, and the children came running from the gardens to find out what all the noise was about. Shahbano shook off her arm and turned her back on her husband while she ushered the children inside the house. She called for Zainab and ran to the washbasin to pour cold water on her reddened face. Zainab came quickly, concerned by the look on her mistress's face.

"Please bring me some water, Zainab," she said, her voice shaky. Shahbano then went to her study, where, besides her children, her writing desk and books were the only salvation she had. She could not think of any way out of this barbaric situation. She sat quietly with her eyes closed, gathering her thoughts between sips of water.

After writing a few verses of her latest poem, she managed to calm down and decided to come out into the courtyard. It was a warm summer afternoon, and the children had been out playing all day, so they finally went down for a late nap. The cook would be preparing the afternoon tea soon and then the dinner hour and then, finally, sleep, she thought. All the same routines all these years, and nothing much had changed. She felt that she was changing with time but in another direction, not one that was aligned with this house. A parallel shift was occurring, like a continental drift. Where this shifting and moving would bring her, she had no answer to.

The house was quiet as she circled the fountain and listened to the musical sound of the water as it splashed onto to the mosaic tiles. The fragrance of the jasmine bushes surrounding the courtyard was drifting slowly into her senses. She took a deep breath as the night sky formed its infusions of purple hazes across the horizon.

There was a shuffling sound that she heard suddenly, coming from the west corridor that led to the other side rooms. And then, suddenly, she heard the sound of a door shutting hard. She and her husband had moved into separate bedrooms almost in the first few months of their marriage. She had insisted on this, though it did not stop him from coming to her whenever he desired, which had ceased in the last year or so. It was his room, she was sure.

She walked down the hall with trepidation and slowly turned the door handle. Then she pushed open the screen door.

Chanda was there. Her kurta was half buttoned, and her face looked flushed. She quickly turned her back to Shahbano and pretended to wipe down his dresser with her dopatta while she buttoned up.

"Oh, Begum Sahiba. I was just making sure the rooms were cleaned properly for the evening, and the beds…"

Shahbano looked over at the bed and saw that the sheets were in a tangle. The beds were made every morning, and the nawab rarely took afternoon naps. She could not have imagined that this—this nagging tug in her gut—could have gone so awry so quickly.

How could he do this in our home? And with the servant girl? She was simultaneously annoyed and shocked.

"Leave. Now!" she shouted. She did not trust herself with the girl at this moment. She might have pulled her hair out or slapped her into oblivion.

The girl darted out of the room quickly, leaving a whiff of something familiar and strange behind that Shahbano had forgotten about. It made her stomach turn, and something in her heart lurched with a sting that made her collapse to the ground.

She took a few deep breaths and then pulled herself up. She went to her bedroom and closed the shutters. She lay there quietly until she heard a knock on the door.

"Shahbano Begum, I need to speak with you," the nawab spoke loudly.

She pulled herself up and straightened her stance. The anger turned to something else, and she knew what she must do.

This was her husband, not the nawab of Khayldi, not the landowner of the china mines or the teak forest but the father of her children, the man she vowed in marriage to, the man who took her for his second wife. *And now this man is fornicating with a servant girl in my house*, she thought.

He walked in, looming large over her slight frame, standing next to the bed they should have shared. "I need your permission, my wife. I would like to marry Chanda and have her live here with us. I know it is not right that I am having relations with her, but she is the right person for me to help manage this land, and I need her with me."

Shahbano slowly circled the room and then stood in front of him, her face still flushed with the memory of the girl's disheveled state. There was a silence between them that hung so heavily, like pregnant clouds before a storm.

She walked over to the dresser, looking at her own reflection. Was it only nine years ago that they looked at each other in that reflecting mirror for the first time? How innocent and naive she had been, she thought. And now here he was ready to move on, to have this village girl sleep in his bed and then take her for his wife and live in their house, with their children calling her Second Mother, or *Choti Amma*.

"Never. No, no, and no. I will not let you bring that jungle whore…that…person… into my house and live here with me and with my precious children. I do not agree to this marriage. I do not give my consent."

The finality of her words gave her strength to continue. They were coming from a place that had lain dormant for many years in some hollow abyss, taking the abuse and the pain and letting it build into this stone mountain that now must never move from its place in her center core.

"You are being ridiculous. Nothing else will change. You can continue living here with the children."

She just glared at him, shocked by his apathy and self-absorption. Though all the signs were there, she never knew it would come to this.

"I would rather live in one of the mud huts on the land than spend one minute being discarded like this. Absolutely not. I do not give my consent."

"Very well then. I will build her another house. She does not have to stay here, but I will marry her, with or without your consent."

Shahbano flipped around and stared at him, not believing what she had just heard.

"How dare you even contemplate such an act. If you continue this nonsense, I will leave with the children, and you will be fortunate if you ever see us again." Her words, her voice, were flowing like lava after an eruption even though her legs and knees were shaking and beginning to wobble. She grabbed the post of the bed and continued, "You have until tomorrow morning to dismiss her and send her back from where she came. And if you choose otherwise, we will be packed and leaving within two days."

He stared at her in what seemed to Shahbano like disbelief. "This is your choice. I have given you a viable option, and you are choosing to break up the family. You will regret it."

He walked away and never came back to her. His decision was made, as was hers. She thought that if he had, even for an inkling, thought to come and discuss something about this with her—the children, her own thoughts, anything—she may have hesitated. It was too much to expect, she knew. She also knew that his elevated position and ability to leverage her and any woman he desired to keep was paramount to the humanity required by him to show compassion and be just.

No wonder Anjuman Bai was so eager to be rid of him. Shahbano realized then that she would never win this battle, that no matter how much she wished, his framework was embedded with a cancer that ate away at men's souls, empowered by a system that kept feeding him a false cure.

That night, she sent a messenger to the bookseller and fellow poets who had been helping her get published to arrange funds for whatever proceeds came from her recent books of poetry to be sent to her father's house. She gathered her jewelry and the coins that she had been saving over the years, as her mother had taught her. Then she went to the safe to find her papers and the *nikkah namah* (or marriage certificate) that stated how much the *haq maher* was for her husband to pay her in case she chose to separate and/or divorce from him, as required by Islamic law. It was a substantial amount, she knew, and he would not argue as the lands and mines were doing well, and he followed the laws of his religion piously. At least, she had that on her side. That was all she wanted from him—nothing more and nothing less.

He did not even mention the children. He hardly knew them or spent time with them. She had her own earnings, and she would manage on that. Any additional money from him was not sacred to her. As far as she was concerned, it was tainted with his own lack of compassion and respect for her as a human being and as a woman, and there would always be strings. She was determined now to find her own way with her children, God willing.

Her breath became steady, and her mind cleared. There was no going back now. Here was another journey, another unknown destination, and she was ready. Finally, she knew in her heart which direction all that incremental shifting was leading her. She had to create her own continent.

The Mountains, Swat Valley (2015)

Finally, they were on their way. The trip began with the flight from Karachi to Islamabad, spending one night in the capital city at Zaina's cousins' home. Travel to Swat began by early dawn, and the bags were already installed in the back of the large white commuter vehicle that her father had leased for the trip.

In the van—which bustling with cousins, aunts, and uncles—Zaina looked out the window at the terraced rice fields and the lush green terrain whizzing by her like a Discovery channel special. This was truly God's world. The people had so little in material possessions, yet they seemed so content and happy.

The van stopped twice on the eight-hour drive: once for tea at the local tea stands and another for breakfast. Her mother and aunts always packed food for the trip, but to Zaina, the best part of traveling to Swat were the food stands along the way. The local paratha and kebab vendors made everything right there in front of you, and the savory and charcoaled aromas were something that alerted her senses to the adventures ahead.

When they finally reached the part where everyone disembarked from the vehicles and prepared for the hike through the mountain terrain, Zaina was filled with exuberance and energy. There were several trackers and helpers who were carrying large woven baskets of food, water, and their luggage alongside; this was assured to make the five-mile trek as comfortable as possible.'

There was a lot of time to chat and spend time and catch up with her cousins and family. This was rare in Karachi as there were always parties or excursions to go crabbing or eat out at a new restaurant. Now, with all of them clad in jeans and sneakers, no fancy hair or makeup, the conversations were deep and real, which was something that Zaina loved. Something about hiking through the natural beauty of this earth brought out the deeper questions of life—a meditative state, almost.

After a few hours, it was time to take a break for tea and snacks. The cook had packed sandwiches for them along with fruits and a few large flasks of tea. When she paused to look around and take a sip of water from the bottle in her backpack, she could see the largest of the mountains in the distance. The sand-colored *Y* shape was distinctively carved into it, and that was their destination. There would be another four hours or so, and with a few breaks in between, they could cool off their faces in the running streams or stop for another break.

At last, they finally arrived at the entrance to the main house. The summer sun was usually milder in the mountains, but the heat was now causing Zaina to yearn for a nice shower and a change of clothes.

Back in the mid-sixties, her uncle had been the head of the Engineering Department at the university, so he was able to wrangle his students to come up with designs and build the retreat with running water and flushing toilets from the surrounding resources. It was truly a miracle to experience such luxury in this oasis.

The stone steps leading up to the front veranda of the bungalow-style stucco and red-tiled house were first intercepted by a natural spring-water fountain cut out of the mountain rock. The spouting water greeted tired and thirsty visitors as they entered the estate. This was pure mineral water, a *chushma* (meaning "clear glass") that was flowing down from the mountains. And as Zaina recalls, it was always very sweet. In fact, she has never had water that tasted so good anywhere else.

Now one could surmise that after hiking for five miles in the hot mountain sun, any water would taste amazing, but everyone knew that there was something very special about that water. There was no question about it.

As she rolled up her jeans to wash her feet, she soaked one end of her cotton dopatta scarf to wipe her face. She was relieved to finally sit for a moment and take in the lush and verdant surroundings.

Everyone was rushing up to the main house to unpack their bags and meet the family and especially to see her uncle—or "Babajan," as everyone called him.

"Come, Zaina. We are all going to go wash up and change so we can meet everyone for dinner at the main house," urged Bina.

There were a few smaller houses that were to accommodate guests as this was a place where not only the family congregated. People from all over the world came to meet her uncle or simply to take in the beautiful scenery while learning and exchanging spiritual ideas and philosophies. It was an interesting mix of family home and spiritual retreat, she supposed, if she had to describe it.

She remembered sitting out on the large tiled terrace in the evenings, as if in a planetarium, the night sky brilliantly lit up, encompassing the mountains. Every star and constellation was so clear and bright.

Her uncle would be speaking to a small gathering of students and scholars. She would just enjoy the sound of his voice, so beautiful and calm, speaking on a variety of topics, some of which were over her head. She was staring into the fountain of mineral water and thinking about how lucky she was to have this beautiful place to come to when she suddenly felt the presence of someone approaching her.

"A penny for your thoughts or, at today's exchange, maybe a hundred rupees?"

The voice was pleasant, and when Zaina looked up, she realized that the face perfectly matched the owner of that lyrical tone.

She looked up and gave a shrug. "Ah well, make that in dollars for me," Zaina replied as she lifted herself up from the stone she was sitting on, realizing that her jeans were caked in mud, and her hair was strewn about. Her cotton kurta was also soaked through from washing her face, so she really was not in any state to meet this annoyingly good-looking stranger.

He was tall and slim, and he must have been a few years older than her, she assumed.

He was sporting a backpack and had on weathered jeans, a faded green T-shirt, and hiking boots. "Hope you had a good hike up here. It's getting easier for me every time I come."

"Uh, yes. The hike was good, but I really should catch up with them." She nodded toward the rest of the crowd as she made her way up the steps. But at the same time, she was feeling a strange pull to actually stay there and talk to him.

"Oh, sure. Of course. I'm Sahil, by the way. Did you come in from the States? Couldn't help but notice an accent and the dollar remark."

As she turned to answer him, her sneakers in hand and barefoot, she ended up missing a step and faltered, trying desperately to grab one of the rocks on the side wall. Sahil quickly caught her elbow and gently put his hand on her back to keep her from crashing into the slate rock wall behind her.

As she found her balance, she realized his hand was still on her arm. Her face obviously flushed, and she was most likely finally feeling the exhaustion of the long trek. "Oh, wow. Thanks so much. I must be more out of it than I thought. Better get to the house and wash up and take a break," she mumbled to break the silence.

The fact was, she was not sure, but she could swear that there was a moment when he caught her that they exchanged glances, and time just stood still—like the universe stopped, and it was just the two of them. It could have been for only a few seconds. Or was it a few minutes? No way to be sure about this.

Could time just stand still? she thought. She had never felt anything like that before.

He slowly let go as she found her balance, and he then agreed that she probably needed to rest. "I was headed down for a short hike. I'm meeting my friends at the big bat cave, so I will probably see you later." He smiled, and Zaina was not sure if this was a question or a comment.

"Oh, that's always a great adventure. Have fun!" She smiled but then quickly darted up the steps to the house before he could reply.

One thing that was certain though was that she could not ignore the sweet buzzing in her head and the feeling that she was perfectly aligned to be in this magical place at this time, right now.

The next day, after recovering from her awkward encounter, she and her cousin Bina were meandering through the estate, admiring all the various foliage and her uncle's cactus collection, when she ran into Sahil again. He was coming down the steps from the library and saw her.

"Hey, dollar Rama. How are you?" he yelled out.

Bina looked over at Zaina with a shocked expression and whispered, "Who is *that*?"

Before Zaina could answer, he had come up to them and was introducing himself. He looked over at Zaina. "I realized that I never got your name." Then, turning to Bina, he said, "I am Sahil, by the way."

"Hi, Sahil. I'm Bina." Her cousin smiled widely and looked ridiculously besotted.

Zaina couldn't help but smile and quipped, "Aka, Batman." She said this to Bina but was looking directly at Sahil, surprising herself by sounding unusually flirtatious.

Bina's eyes widened. "Oh, so this is Batman!"

He quickly laughed and responded, "Touché. So we are on nicknames already? Okay! Who knew hiking the bat caves could bring out the standup comedian in some people, right?"

"By the way, her name is Zaina. Nice to meet you, Sahil."

It was apparent to Zaina that this chance meeting was very likely to disrupt her Zen-like moments here and was very different than her previous Shangri-La summers. Strangely enough, she found it more a comfort than an interruption now. As much as his annoying nickname for her was quite brazen, considering they had just met once, she liked that he got her humor. And, oh, crap, his laugh was making her turn all kinds of stupid.

The next several days were filled with late-night talks on the veranda with Babajan and others. There were hikes to the caves, swimming in the clear mountain pools, and picnics where the food was cooked on small stoves on the rocks. The evening meals were usually a big affair with all the family and guests present. The large dining hall and table were laid properly, and food was brought out by the helpers from the kitchen.

She looked forward to running into him at these gatherings and started making note of his whereabouts more carefully. He had a group of friends, and they all had great respect for these surroundings and especially for her uncle. There was always something to talk and laugh about as everyone shared their day's experiences over dessert and chai. Then all wandered onto the various terraces, the library to read, or other areas of the estate to tell stories or just hang out.

If she got up early enough, Zaina would wander the estate, and she often would go to the kitchen, where Hoori (the cook) would begin preparing the morning meal. She would smile and make a special *meetha paratha* for her with a strong cup of *pakki pakai* chai while stirring pots and scurrying about the stone hearth and stove. Her name, *Hoori*, meant "fairy," and she reminded Zaina of the plump blue fairy godmother in *Sleeping Beauty*. Was it Fauna or Flora? She couldn't remember for sure, but she had the same wide gleeful smile and sparkling eyes along with what seemed like magical powers in the way she conjured up amazing meals for as many as forty to fifty guests at a time. Her warmth and obvious love for this place could be deceiving though. She was a tough cookie and kept all the servants in line. No one disobeyed her as she almost ran the place.

There was also Dimitris, the caretaker, who would just show up, seemingly out of nowhere, when Hoori called out his name to run an errand or fix something in the kitchen. One could not tell his age because he looked like an old man but could lift the eighty-pound bags of grain with ease or run up and down the mountain to catch the goats faster than the young boys who ran after him. His fair skin, blue eyes, and sandy-colored hair likened him to a European. These traits were not questioned, for it was well known that he was descended directly from Alexander the Great (or Sikander, as he was known in these parts) when the area was invaded by those battalions and armies centuries ago. For Zaina, it struck as serendipitous that the great military leader was taught by Aristotle in philosophy, medicine, and science—some subjects that her uncle now shared his knowledge about with visitors to this place.

She had observed for a while now that for all the machismo in Pathan culture, she couldn't help but notice that the women were the ones who really ruled the roost. They seemed to have a strength and determination that was underplayed for cultural reasons. Staying subservient to men was a more feminine and subsequently more attractive quality, especially to attract a husband who preferred to control his wife. Perhaps that was why the Pathan men who degraded women felt so threatened by them that they had to keep them uneducated and under purdah. When given the freedom to choose their own destiny and path, they excelled with intelligence and drive. That intensity was kept in check not only to suppress their success but also because, combined with their beauty, it was a triple threat to the egocentric male-dominant society to see such female ferocity. It was a rare man that could uphold such gifts in a woman, especially in these parts.

In her own family, Zaina had many such success stories of brilliant women going into medicine, law, and engineering. Not to mention powerful businesswomen and politicians. Even then, the women upheld their own in the home by caring for the children and looking after the household. That was the price they paid for their freedom. Those cultural norms would take more than a few generations to adapt until a woman was allowed to just exist without exceptions, until she no longer needed the approval of society or men.

Hoori did not have the education or chances to explore any other life, but something told Zaina that even if she had, she would not have opted for anything else than being here. Her whip-smart intelligence and wit shone in her eyes, and she worked like a gladiator from early morning to late into the night. The kitchen was her domain, and no one could make a move there without her approval.

She had been training her daughter, Sobia, from a young age to learn all that she knew so that one day, when the time came, there would be no gap in the caretaking of the household duties as serving Babajan and his followers was her honor and pride. She revered Zaina's uncle like a brother, as he did her. They were family and well protected and cared for through the generations.

Hoori knew all the comings and goings here. Like the guardian of a fort, she knew who to trust and who to keep at a distance. She prayed with everyone on Fridays and relied on the good wishes of all who came through this mountain retreat, and many came through. Some stayed longer than others, but they all knew who she was. Zaina's uncle made sure of that.

She had often heard that you could tell the humanity of a person by the way they treated the helpers (or subordinates) and children in their environment. Babajan was a true example of this, and he always introduced Hoori and his helpers to everyone. He asked after them and listened patiently to the children's stories. He loved the innocence of children and would often break out in a bellowing laugh at their jokes or comments.

Early one morning, Zaina came to Hoori's kitchen, and all was quiet. She looked around, and though a few pots were simmering, Hoori was nowhere in sight. She walked a bit farther up and wandered onto a path that led to some rocks and then the small pool that was fed by water from the mountaintop.

She saw Hoori sitting by one of the rocks and holding her hands spread wide. She was murmuring a prayer.

Zaina waited but Hoori heard the rustle of her feet and turned around. She smiled and motioned for her to come near.

"I am so sorry, Hoori. I did not want to disturb you."

"Don't be crazy, Zaina jaan. I was just thanking Allah for all that he has given me. I am glad to see you. How about some chai and a paratha?" Her voice was softer now, and Zaina noticed a moistness in her eyes.

"No, no, it's fine. I just didn't see you in the kitchen, so I was wondering where you were."

She motioned again for Zaina to sit by her. "There has been no delivery of supplies this morning, and I am a bit short, so I am trying to do the best I can since we have so many guests staying on now."

"Can I help? We can send some of the guys down to the town to get a few things."

Hoori just smiled and shook her head. "Let me tell you something, Zaina jaan. I have never asked for any supplies in all the years I have been here. There was one time, that summer when we had over seventy guests staying, and I kept cooking and cooking until, one day, I came to the kitchen and realized, there was not enough food to feed everyone for the next few days. The supplies come every week, but because of the floods, the helpers could not bring up the supplies to us.

"I just prayed and went back to my room. I didn't want to bother Babajan with this, but somehow, he got word of it and called for me to come and see him. I went with my head hanging down, and he just put his hand on my head and smiled. 'Go back to sleep, Hoori. You have worked so hard. You are tired. God will provide. He sees all.'

"I didn't know what to say, and so I did what he said. I couldn't sleep, so I just stayed in my room. When, after a while, I came back to the kitchen, there were crates of lentils, rice, vegetables, and fruits stacked up on the side wall of the kitchen. Meats were stored in ice near the sink, and everything else that I needed was piled on the table here. I do not know what happened or how it happened, but by God's grace, we have never had a shortage of food here. Everyone brings their good wishes to this place, and we never need to ask for anything."

At this point, Zaina's eyes were also welling up with tears. She had heard many such incidents that happened here, and this was one that stayed with her for a long time.

The Cave

There had been rumblings of the Taliban and Al-Qaeda factions of late, men with turbans and rifles coming through the area or the sound of gunshots every now and then. The elders warned the kids to stay close to the main house and to be aware of anything or anyone that looked suspicious. This was especially true for the girls and women as they had to cover their heads when they saw a stranger or look away. Apparently, the days of women freely walking the area alone without male escorts were, sadly, long gone.

Meeting Sahil was, for Zaina, the icing on the cake of this trip. Now there was a new layer of excitement and joy in her demeanor as she meandered about. Her cousins had to shake her out of it from time to time, and she knew it was so out of character for her to be this lost and absent-minded. For some unexplainable reason, she could sense his presence even before she saw him, entering a room or taking a walk with her cousins.

There were late-night forays to the waterfalls, their eyes locking over a cup of tea or a shared moment. Their conversations varied from politics to his work at the university, her art, his disdain for the Dadaists and her love of them, and his passion for Billy Joel songs (which they both agreed on). They argued about big government vs. NGOs and homeschooling vs. public education. He played the guitar and had managed to give a nightly show, which everyone enjoyed. His rendition of Billy Joel's "She's Always a Woman" was beautiful, and Frank Sinatra's "Strangers in the Night" was a surprise.

They laughed and flirted, and on occasion, their eyes would meet, and she could not turn away. This wasn't the first boy that she had been infatuated with or even gone out with. At college, she had many opportunities to meet and mingle with guys. But this was on another level. There was something of her that merged with him, which she had never experienced before.

On the last night before Sahil was leaving, he asked her to take a small walk with him after dinner. She did not see any harm with that, except that she was not sure what the others would say.

"Sure, let me get Bina," she replied quickly, not wanting to set off any alarms with her mother or aunts. But her inside voice said, *Just go with him. What are you waiting for?*

"Wait. I just want to talk to you, Zaina. Alone."

She sensed an urgency in his voice and, not sure why, she replied, "Okay, sure. But umm…"

She didn't know how to tell him that it was really not appropriate because, in her heart, she did want to spend some time alone with him. This had been the most exhilarating time for her, and being with Sahil made her feel something that was missing in her life. He was in her soul, and every time she saw him or was around him, her soul danced.

The strange part is that she didn't even know she had a part of her that was incomplete—that she even needed completion.

How many times had she seen or heard about such feelings, that romantic haze that came over people? She brushed it off as chick lit or for girls with fantasies of Prince Charming's scooping them off their feet. But this was real, as real as her racing heart every time she saw him, and it was nothing that she could have thought possible.

She had a good life and good friends, but now, to go back to it seemed like going back to black and white after falling into a rainbow. Was it just that maybe she didn't realize how mediocre her life had been? The more she tried to filter and understand, the less she could resolve it in her mind. She wished there was some sign or magic formula that would give her the answer. She had never felt stronger about anything in her gut than this.

Sahil quickly attempted to alleviate her apprehension. "I know. I understand how this might look, but I told your cousins, and they are okay with it. They will cover for us if need be."

With just these few words, he was able to convince her. This was something she never could have imagined. She didn't trust so easily, and her instincts had always served her well.

She smiled and took a step back, tilting her head to one side. "Oh, really?" She couldn't resist the urge to tease him. "I see. Did you get Alfred to ready the Batmobile and set up the getaway too?" She was feeling quite amused and impressed that he had thought and planned this far ahead.

He too smiled and then looked upward and laughed, the kind of sound that made her chest tighten and skip a beat. "Ha ha. Just come with me, Dollar Dolly."

He gently took her hand and started on a trail that he was obviously familiar with. At this point, she thought helplessly, she would have followed him to the ends of the earth.

They had walked through some of the brush and thickets for about ten minutes. They did not speak, just held hands and walked in silence. The air between them was filled with something that did not need words, a quiet understanding that each was communicating through a wavelength of connected rays.

He had managed to finagle a lantern from the watchman, and they came to an open area where there was an entrance to a small opening to what looked like a cave. Now Zaina knew there were many caves on the property because they had gone cave hiking quite often. She had not seen this one before. It was much easier to get to, and it was strange that she had never been here, perhaps due to the overgrown foliage hanging in front of it.

Sahil lifted the lantern and motioned for Zaina to move forward. She looked at him quizzically and would have questioned anyone else's motives at this point. But somehow, she completely trusted him.

Inside, she saw that some colorful tribal rugs had been laid with throw pillows. There was a pot of tea and what looked like s'mores on a plate. She must have mentioned that as a Girl Scout, her favorite part of camping was having s'mores by the fire.

Her eyes widened, and her smile gave him the response he was aiming for. "Are you kidding me? Where and how did you get s'mores all the way up here in the middle of the Swat Valley?"

"Hah. So I did my homework. The driver knows some locals in town, and I just had to bribe him with my Nike T-shirt and a pouch of coffee. Come on. Will Mademoiselle please have a seat?" He said this while bowing and motioning his arm like a ballet dancer.

At this display, Zaina burst into a laugh that she usually saved for girls' night or pajama parties. She did not know what to make of the grand gesture but was now in a state of complete joy. She curled up on the floor cushions, hugging her knees and smiling broadly. To have Sahil all to herself, here with this spread, in a beautiful and secluded spot on a mountain, her most favorite place on earth, was heaven.

"You are the best," she said, managing a smile as she looked up at him. Her eyes started to moisten, catching the rays of the firelight in the lantern.

"Are you okay, Zaina? What's the matter?"

She looked down as a tear slipped from her eye and slid down her cheek. "I am so sorry, Sahil. This is the kindest, most thoughtful thing anyone has ever done for me. I am the one always coming up with special gifts and events for all my friends and family, but you are the first person who really found my soul. Thank you. I will never forget this night."

His childlike smile and bright eyes shone as he inched to give her a kiss on the cheek. "If this is all it takes, I hope I can give you a lifetime of s'mores, my darling Zaina."

Her name on his lips was like honey. Did she ever really hear her name before?

They sat there in silence, a quiet hum of synergy between them that needed no words. She leaned on his shoulder, the faraway sounds of crickets chirping to the beats of their hearts. Then she gently pulled him away and touched his face, memorizing each line and crevice.

He wanted to take her into his arms but hesitated. Suddenly, he jolted up as they heard a loud bang, distant but very loud. The ferocity of the pounding blast rattled them both out of their elusive bubble.

The Descent

They both reacted at the same time. The first sound was vaguely familiar, and then she heard the gunshots repeat and get louder.

Sahil jerked his head around and put his hand on her mouth. "Shhh…don't move."

They moved deeper into the cave as they heard more gunshots and men shouting in Pashto. Sahil put out the lantern. There were screams and much scuffling above at the main house.

Zaina wanted to run out and see if her parents and family were safe, but she knew that there were armed guards and watchmen as well as many family members who were well versed in armed protection for this area. She closed her eyes and prayed, a slow terror beginning to seep into her.

"I know Pushto," Sahil whispered as she put her hand in his tightly. They are just doing a raid to make sure there are no American spies here. We are better off in this cave right now." He also said some prayers then brushed his hand over her head and kissed her forehead.

They huddled together, and under any other circumstances, she would have embraced each moment with him, allowing herself to get lost in his embrace, the rough feel of his beard against her face, the slight scent of aftershave, and his warm breath. But now, only fear and uncertainty coursed through her veins as she clung to him for safety. *Sahil*, she thought of the meaning of his name, *the safe shore of the ocean*.

Zaina was not sure how long they had been there. She may have drifted off to sleep a few times, but when she awoke, finally, the early morning light began to drift into the cave, and she saw Sahil asleep. For the first time, she could stare at him without his knowing. His long lashes were splayed on fine cheekbones and a single mole on one side. His thick hair was disheveled and a shade of deep brown, and his cotton chambray shirt was crumpled.

She was startled into reality as she remembered the previous night's events. She had to see what was going on. She started to get up and creep toward the entrance of the cave when she felt a hand pulling her back by the waist.

"Wait, Zaina. Don't go out yet. I will check and see what is going on."

His voice was low and hoarse. She wondered if he had been up most of the night. He had jumped up when he saw her and was now in a state of red alert. His hand was still on her waist, and she turned toward him, their faces just inches apart. She looked directly in his eyes and held his arm, and he seemed startled but drawn in.

"Sahil, whatever happens, I will always be grateful to you for this," she said and softly kissed his cheek, resting her face on his for just a moment.

He held her tightly and wondered what their chances of getting out of this mess alive would be, and if he would ever see her again if they made it. He whispered in her ear, "Daa tor makh de wrak sha."

She stared at him with a questioning look on her face.

"It's in Pushto, but I want you to remember it. 'I love everything about you except your absence.'"

When they emerged from the cave, they were startled to find that the whole estate had been evacuated. Sahil had taken the first round of inspections then came and got Zaina. No one was around. It was very eerie to see empty rooms and books left where they were and food on the table, untouched, where there had been so much life. They were both dumbstruck as to what could have happened. It was just one night. At least, there were no bodies or injured persons, they surmised.

Zaina began to panic and went to the bedrooms of the main house, where she had been staying with her mother and cousins. The bags were all gone, sheets turned out, and closet doors were left ajar, emptied of their contents.

Zaina searched around for anything that would give her a clue or trace of what to do or where to go from here. She went to her bed and slumped down. Then she felt something under her, pinching. She lifted the mattress from the springs underneath and found a pillowcase stuffed hastily with her personal toiletries. Her toothbrush, its holder, toothpaste, a bar of lavender soap, her hairbrush, and her travel-size bottle of Advil. Only her mother could have known how much she would need these.

That is odd, she thought. *Why is my toothbrush out of the holder?*

As she pried open the toothbrush holder, she found five, one hundred-dollar bills rolled tightly in there.

"Sahil, what is going on?" Her voice was shaking now. "Where is my family? And where is everyone?"

He seemed as confused and lost as she was. "Okay, let's try to figure out what to do next. The only explanation that makes any sense is that there was some kind of a raid here and, God forbid, they were all kidnapped or…" He stopped, seeing the look of dread starting to spread on her face, and immediately added, "More likely, they decided to clear out after some sort of scuffle."

He paused and looked around. The serene beauty and peace of this majestic retreat was taking on an eerie quality that made him very uneasy. "But why they left in such a rush and without us is the question," he added, almost to himself.

"I found a few of my things and this money." She showed him the bills. "All my other things were gone, even the suitcases and books I brought with me. Except these two, which I had hidden from my cousins on top of the cabinet here. They always borrow my books and never put them back."

"What books did you bring? What about your passport or other picture ID?"

She told him that, luckily, her uncle had kept all those in a safe in his home in Karachi and advised not to carry them with her since there was always a chance of them getting lost or stolen.

"Oh, that was a smart move," he said approvingly. He held up the books she had pulled out. "Edith Wharton and Candace Bushnell. What is this, *Downton Abbey* meets *Sex and the City*? Really?"

He smiled for the first time, and she smiled back. She forgot how funny he could be. "I am not sure what bothers me more about that question—that you know about *Downton Abbey* or that you watched *Sex and the City*," she replied in defense.

"Okay, okay," he conceded, becoming serious again. "American authors can be a trigger. As for the money, I think your mother or someone who knew you would find it left it there to help you try to get out of here. But it is dollars, not rupees." He said this with a low murmur, as if going through the details of how they could manage to navigate their way back to the city and their families.

"What difference does that make?" Zaina asked him, again confused but wanting to understand what kind of a plan he was coming up with. She was a planner too and did not leave much to fate or surprises in her life, though this was one of those times that would challenge her need to be in control.

"Anything indicating that there were foreigners here, especially American, could cause alarm. I will try to convert some of the money along the way, if possible, if it's okay with you."

She nodded, glad that he refrained from making any dollar jokes.

They walked around through the estate, looking for any signs that may indicate something to help solve this strange situation. When they were passing the small mosque in the center with its gardens of roses and bright pink bougainvillea wrapped around the pillars at the entrance, Zaina stopped. "Wait here, Sahil. I need to collect my tasbih. I left it here when I came a few days ago."

He nodded as she went inside, and he heard a loud gasp. Zaina couldn't believe her eyes. The beautiful portraits of the saints that were so revered and had been displayed at the small entrance before going into the prayer area had been smashed and thrown down on the ground. Her eyes filled with tears as she began to pick them up.

"Stop. Please don't touch these or try to fix this mess. When the authorities come, they will have to see the motivation behind this raid and go after the suspects with this evidence. I know it is disturbing, but it is a clear sign to me of who is responsible now."

Zaina nodded slowly then took off her shoes and went into the prayer room. There were some shelves with books, Qurans and chapters for those that wanted to sit and read or recite, and a bowl of prayer beads. She had left her prayer beads next to the bowl and collected the string now, which was made of tiger's-eye and ebony, wrapping it around her wrist. She remembered that Babajan had once seen these and remarked how beautiful they were. She had offered the strand to him, but he simply placed them in his hand, and as he admired them, he murmured something she did not hear and put them back into her palm, placing his hand around her closed fist for a few seconds. She did not know what to make of this gesture, but nothing done by him was small or insignificant, so she cherished these beads with all her heart.

By this time, Sahil had already started to lay out a strategy and told her to come with him to the servants' quarters up on the far side of the estate. There were a few small hutlike structures built into the mountain terrain, all void of any persons, yet still, one could smell the coals and earthy dampness that must have been from the cooking and washing there the night before.

He rummaged around until he found a plain wool chador and hat for himself and a printed cotton shawl for her. He also found a woman's shalwar and kurta, which he instructed her to change into from her jeans and shirt.

Zaina looked around at the small, cloistered space where a whole family may have lived and thought about her expansive home in the States, about running a hot shower whenever she wanted or going out to eat at a nice restaurant. How little these people needed to be happy, and yet even this small peace was threatened now. Her heart sank at the sadness and emptiness of this place that had seen so many beautiful and happy times.

There were some beaten leather male sandals that Sahil slipped on while she changed. He then found a pair for her as well. "We need to get out of here without attracting any attention. You need to keep this chador on your head and stay a few paces behind me. I know this is going to be tough, Zaina, but believe me, this is the only way we can try to get back to Islamabad and get to the bottom of this. You can be my wife or my sister...up to you." He cleared his throat, and his voice stumbled a bit at this.

"Wife," Zaina blurted, startled at her own forthrightness.

He nodded but kept going, "Your family is from Hazara, and my family is from Peshawar. I speak Pushto and will answer all the questions. If they talk to you, just look down. Under no circumstances can you look any of the men in the eyes. Zaina, this is very important...or speak any English. I can deal with them, but I need you to do your part."

She just looked at him and was overwhelmed by all this information and his adept call to action in forming the plan. "Of course, I get it. I grew up in America, but I know this part of the world is very different and how these tribal Pathans can be."

She spoke with confidence, not wanting him to doubt her ability to help them escape from this fiasco or to know how scared she really was. Her mind was racing to the events of the night before, and her heart felt heavy with thoughts of whether her family made it safely out of there.

Tears began to well up in her eyes, and she quickly blinked them away. But not before she caught Sahil looking at her in a way that no other person she knew, ever before, could make her whole existence seem justified.

His face softened, and he gently dabbed her face with his thumb and held her for a few minutes before they began their trek down the mountain. "Okay. Let's do this."

Zaina: The Return

Going back to Islamabad, then to Karachi, and finally taking the flight the next day to the States, Zaina was grateful to get back home. There was something about Sahil that was tugging at her, and she couldn't stop thinking about him.

She didn't even have time to get his contact information. It was just a blur now, her family quickly whisking her back to Karachi then catching the next flight to the States. The unbelievable experience and journey of theirs back to the city from the mountainous terrain, with all the dangers of the extremist factions there, was something she would never forget. His immediate command of the situation and cool demeanor as they were interrogated by bearded strangers swinging Kalashnikovs managed to make her feel safe.

And for some reason, she was very proud of him. She hardly knew the guy, but fate had brought them together in that magical place in the stars and then tested their trust in each other with the dangerous trek back to civilization.

This was how Zaina saw it. This was what her grandmother was talking about, and she felt something both wonderful and terrifying in the depths of her heart. There were always so many people around that summer, but his presence pierced at her through all the others. He had told her that he was teaching and doing his doctorate at the university close to her hometown. So strange that they never met there but instead at a place hardly anyone knew about on the other side of the world.

Somehow, she would have to convince her mother about continuing with her graduate work and to join the curator program there as soon as she got back. This would buy some time. Her father would be the key. He was the catalyst behind anything that his children wanted to do with education. Luckily, he saw no difference between his sons and daughters when it came to higher learning and careers.

Time was running at a strange speed nowadays for Zaina. Was it just a month or a few weeks ago that she had thought she could meet Sahil again? They had probably passed by each other on campus several times, never noticing or connecting, and now she was getting anxious as to how to find him. Why didn't she get his contact information? Even an email, something, anything, she thought. Did she just imagine him?

Her simple dilemma started to take on a new dimension. Zaina could not find out exactly where Sahil was at the university. She had managed to get into the graduate program there and work part-time at the museum. This was one challenge that she had to wrestle out of her mother. And when her parents saw that she was serious, she simply had to hold her ground and keep looking ahead.

The marriage proposals and would-be suitors needed to be quashed. Zaina knew what she wanted now, and nothing else compared to what she had in mind. Fighting the good fight was not easy. Her mother refused to talk to her for days, and her father looked apologetic over his cups of tea or at the dinner table. She even tried to get Shahana's mother to mediate the issue, but unfortunately, Shae was marrying the chosen prince her mother wanted, so no points on Zaina's side there.

It should not be this hard to locate someone. After all, we have the internet, Google, and LinkedIn, she thought. But for some reason, the name that she had did not fit any of the profiles that Sahil had mentioned to her. She didn't even have his address in Pakistan, of his family, that she could try and contact.

How had things gone so wrong? she thought. *How was everything left so awry?*

This angst and lingering feeling of wanting to find the answers, yet unsure as to how, became part of Zaina's daily quest and ritual. She would get up at 6:00 a.m. every day, go for her run or to the gym, have a quick shower, and dress for the day. Breakfast consisted of a fruit smoothie or a protein bar. The university was about thirty minutes away, so she got there around eight thirty, and she would usually grab a coffee at Einstein's Café. Her classes were three days a week and started at 10:00 a.m. The rest of the week was to finish her papers or put in her hours at the gallery.

This routine gave her enough time to set up her laptop or go to the library and start her daily search. She even searched the databases at the university. He said he was teaching while doing his doctorate in the Nuclear Engineering Department. What was most baffling to Zaina was that no one had heard his name.

How is that possible? she thought.

One day, finally frustrated with the lack of information, Zaina went to the Engineering Building. It was not far from the library and was easy to spot: a large cinder block-style building painted white, with black-edged windows running along the sides. She used her student ID to scan and gain entrance. There was an information desk, and she went there to get some answers.

The girl at the desk had wire-rimmed glasses, and her reddish hair was pulled back in a ponytail. An air of ennui was on her face as she looked up and saw Zaina walk in, but then she quickly went back to scanning her phone.

"Excuse me. Can you please locate a student or doctoral fellow here that I am trying to find?"

The girl looked up from her phone at Zaina as if she was asking for the next shuttle to Mars and droned, "What's the name?"

"Well, that's the problem. I don't think I have the proper name, but he was an assistant professor here and is finishing or maybe finished his master's or PhD with the Nuclear Engineering Department, probably around this year…or next?"

She realized, as she said it, that she sounded like an imbecile. She wished she had prepared or had more information.

"So do you have a name or not?" the girl snapped.

Now, normally, Zaina was the embodiment of grace and diplomacy. She was raised that way, and it mostly worked in her favor. She could smile, politely inquire, and get through any challenging situation with patience and civility. But this girl, at this time, with this situation, was starting to prick at Zaina's sensibilities.

"I do. But as I mentioned, it may not be what you have. His name is Sahil. Sahil Khan or Mazar or Manzoor." She racked her brain for the family name.

Zaina did not want to deal with this person. She didn't seem like she was inclined to be helpful. And anyway, it would be better to just talk to a professor or someone whom he may have worked with.

"Can you please just direct me to the Nuclear Engineering Department? That would be a big help."

Another look of disdain. "You can't just walk into the department. There are security measures. You will need to obtain a pass from an administrator, and no one is here to give that access."

The girl gave another look and started typing S-A-H-E-L.

"No, no. Not *E*. It is with an *I*. Sahil." As she said this, her tone probably sounded louder and more annoyed than she intended.

Just then, an attractive woman with short blond hair walked past them and looked at Zaina in a curious way. For some reason, their eyes connected, and Zaina abruptly took her arm. "Excuse me. I am so sorry to bother you, but I really need to find someone, and I know he worked here or does work here, but I am not sure. Would you know him?"

She was slim but with an athletic build. Her aquamarine-blue eyes shone with intelligence and clarity. She was dressed in a simple navy linen shift with a white tank, tan leather slides, and a delicate gold chain with a small round charm dangling from it, which looked to Zaina like *Kimberly* written in Arabic script.

"Who are you looking for?" she asked distantly, almost with hesitation, as if she didn't want to hear the answer.

"Sahil. He was—or is—a professor here. I am not sure what his last name is. I think he was finishing his doctorate in engineering."

The woman looked at Red, who rolled her eyes in a "good luck, babe, she's all yours" expression, and the blonde just took Zaina's arm and guided her to the lounge area of the lobby. "Let's sit down. You seem very distressed. Is everything all right?"

Zaina continued to pursue her questioning. "Do you know him or know of him? He was here with the Nuclear Engineering Department. Where can I find out how to get in touch with him?"

At this point, Zaina's voice was teetering on breaking down. She could feel the moistness begin to prick her eyes. She had to maintain her composure, but the frustration was getting to her.

The woman did not seem fazed by Zaina's frantic and repetitive inquisitions. "My name is Dr. Kimberly Branson. And you are…?"

"Oh, so sorry. My name is Zaina Qureshi. I am a grad student here. Just started this semester." She had already apologized twice to this woman and was not sure why she felt so uncomfortable with her.

"Nice to meet you. I am one of the engineering professors here. Have been for the last few years, and I am so sorry to tell you that I really have not heard this name before or know of anyone in our faculty of that description."

Zaina's heart took a dive into her stomach, and she visibly slumped back into the sofa.

Dr. Branson looked sympathetically at Zaina and put a hand on hers. "Was he someone close to you?" she asked, talking in the past tense. This was a bit odd to Zaina since she claimed that there was no one here by that description.

"Yes, he was," she answered quietly. Suddenly, she got up, wanting to leave this place. Something was not right, and she needed to get out of here. "Well, thanks so much for your help. I appreciate it." She shook Dr. Branson's hand and swiftly left the building.

She was going to be late for her Far Eastern Antiquities class, so she ran across campus and hurriedly shuffled into one of the chairs at the back of the lecture hall.

Sahil: The Departure

The cell was dark and damp. The stench of urine and decay filled his nostrils as he forced himself up, and the day started like this. He tried to count the days by keeping a tiny piece of bread for each day he had been here. Unfortunately, the mice had no respect for calendars, and so that system was shot. Each time he tried to get the attention of the guard or anyone who came by to let him get a lawyer or make a call, he was given a slap or completely ignored. He was given a mat to sleep on, and the gray shirt and pants they gave him to wear were worn thin by this time.

The prisoners were all shoved in the bathing area at one time and only every few weeks.

It was humiliating, but to Sahil, it was a chance to see and talk to the others. None seemed to have a clue as to why they were brought there—either that or they were not willing to talk. As it was, every time he started to gather some information, a guard would shout profanities at him and beat him with a stick.

There was little he could manage to navigate in this hellhole to find a solution. It was literally "damned if you do, damned if you don't." He tried to cooperate and stay quiet, but then he was completely ignored. He tried to make noise and screamed to get attention, and he was, again, punished by a beating or the withholding of food or water. His skin was beginning to have scabs and scars that did not look like they had any inkling of healing, hanging loosely on his now bony body.

The rough-looking guard, in a shabby khaki uniform, yanked open the lock on the barred cell and pulled Sahil by his hair and threw him against the wall. He could feel his skull scrape and thud against the stone surface as he collapsed to the ground, his eyes blurring and his head pounding. After hitting him with a few more punches, the guard spouted at him, "No one is coming to get you, fool! Just be glad you haven't been tortured yet. This is a picnic for you right now, unless you want to go for a swim!" This was roared through gritted teeth and then followed by a huge laugh.

He must have seen hundreds of guys like me, Sahil thought. *There is no room for humanity or compassion in that soul anymore.*

The guard walked away slowly, rubbing the left side of his face as a bright red blotch began to appear.

"Ali!" someone shouted. "Get over here. We need your help with the new detainees!"

Was it a month, two months, a year? What day was it? What month? All these questions seemed to fall into the abyss that was Sahil's spiraling universe nowadays. He tried to piece together the events that led him here, and none of the sequence made any sense. His memory had a few stark moments as he looked back and tried remembering those to keep his sanity.

* * * * *

He had been hiking with his friends. Flirting and laughing with Zaina and the serene beauty of that place were the few memories that kept him alive and alert. A few days before the attack, when looking around for Zaina, Sahil had come up to the main house. It was midday, so most of the guests were taking their afternoon siesta, and the kitchen was quiet as well. He felt restless and was searching for something to do—maybe go to the library and get a book. He opened one of a set of screen doors that had another solid door behind it. The door was unlocked, so he went in, not realizing that someone was in the room. The room was dark, but he could see that it was Babajan, sitting cross-legged on the floor in his customary white kurta and pajama. His eyes were closed, and for some reason, there was a distinct scent of roses and some strange vibration that Sahil could feel under his feet. "Come in, my son. Sit with me," Sahil heard him say.

"Oh, my apologies, Babajan. I was looking for the library."

"You were looking for something, yes, but it is not in the library. Come."

Sahil, still confused as to how Babajan knew it was him without ever seeing his face, instinctively walked over and sat next to the elderly man. He knew that he must be at least in his late seventies, but his hair was still dark with no visible grays. He did not have a beard like most holy men that Sahil had imagined or seen.

When Babajan turned to look at Sahil, there was a golden glow in his amber eyes, and he spoke slowly, "It will be difficult, but you will manage to come through." He smiled and turned back to center and closed his eyes again.

Sahil was confused. "Sorry, er…I am not sure if you are talking to me."

Babajan was quiet. "Just sit still with me, Sahil. You will need your strength. There will be many trials. Just remember, the one in charge is not your enemy."

Sahil could not say how long he sat there with him. His heart and mind were floating in space as he closed his eyes and let the time pass. Then Babajan placed his hand on Sahil's shoulder and motioned for him to take his leave. "I will rest now. Go enjoy your time with her. She is very special to me." He said this very matter-of-factly, as if they were having a conversation and Sahil was telling him about Zaina. He didn't even mention her name, but they both knew who he was talking about.

How could this person know what was in his heart and even give some guidance for something that Sahil was still trying to figure out? It was truly a transformative moment and maybe one that he would never forget. There was an undeniable surge of energy that he felt when leaving Babajan's room.

Then, back in Islamabad, his mother and family were so relieved to see him. Mukhs recounted the raid in the mountains. How they had to pack up and leave, almost at gunpoint. The extremist rebels were shooting and destroying everything that had to do with the Sufi order and anything that seemed to be connected with Western influences. Those factions of so-called Islamic fundamentalists were against the Sufis because they embraced all faiths and the higher order of God's love, which they proposed came in many forms. The Sufi philosophy was of tolerance and love, but more prominent was its high regard and respect for women. True Islam is in the respect for those who practice charity and love toward each other. Suppressing women and forcing culturally adopted rules of anarchy and misogyny was itself against Islam.

Luckily, the tribal leaders knew of the power of Babajan's strong following in the area and let the guests and family leave without hurting anyone. How he and Zaina managed to escape was nothing short of a miracle; someone was truly looking out for them.

Sahil could not get Zaina out of his mind. That night, in Swat, with the full display of the stars and constellations, and in the cave, he wanted to just hold her and keep her safe. Their near escape from the Taliban attack had been an experience that brought the meandering questions of life and love in his world to a screeching halt. She was posing as his wife, looking demurely down as gun-toting tribesmen would randomly stop them as they made their way down the mountain. Sahil spoke in Pashto, explaining that they were going to the village to see family. Luckily, he had made this trek several times and knew the landmarks and followed the small streams to get to the local village.

There were a few times when she simply stood behind him, quiet. But other times, when the terrain became rocky, she held his hand tight, and he clung to hers as well. She was a good climber, and he appreciated that she never complained of thirst or exhaustion, though he himself had felt it at times. He knew if he could get through that with her, she was truly the kind of partner he wanted to share a life with.

Finally reaching the village, they searched around for a ride to Islamabad. The money was exchanged discreetly so they could pay for the car and driver. They found a small open-air stall and bought some fruits and water to keep and have on the way. Sahil did not want to waste a minute to get back. Surely, they would have some idea of what happened when they got to the big city.

"I hope you can trust this driver," Zaina whispered to Sahil. "We don't know who and where these guys came from."

He just nodded. "Trust me, Zaina. We don't have much choice. We were lucky to get someone to take us today. Otherwise, we would have had to wait until morning for the next available car." Then he looked at her, worried if she would make it the rest of the way back. "Are you okay?" he asked hesitantly. "Stay with me. We will get through this."

She just nodded. *Trust me*, she thought. *That is what I am doing. God only knows why.*

They finally got back to Islamabad, and she contacted her family, who was still there. They came and got her, thanked him, and then she was gone. Just like that. There was no opportunity to exchange emails or phone numbers. Her frantic parents just seemed relieved to find her and take her back as soon as possible. She gave him one long glance and hesitated but was quickly swept away.

"We are going back on the next flight back to Boston," he heard her father say. "This has been too traumatic for you, Zaina. And for us all."

It seemed a hundred lifetimes ago, and yet it could have been yesterday. It was only when he got to his home and was received by his panic-stricken mother and sisters that he realized something was really wrong.

"Sahil, you must hurry. I will speak to my cousin at the airport security. We will book you on the soonest flight we can get." His mother was talking with a strain in her voice that he had not heard before.

"I don't understand. What do you know about what happened there in Swat?"

She quickly put a hand over his mouth and pointed to the ceiling fan. "Your semester will be starting soon. You must return as soon as possible, no?"

Sahil was again apprehensive about his mother's need to be careful as she pointed to what may have been a bug in the room. How could he leave them like this?

She then took a piece of paper and wrote on it. *The police and intelligence-agency people were here looking for you. There is something wrong. You must get back to the US as soon as possible.*

He then understood that he had to leave the country. There was a strange and dangerous tone to his mother's warning, and he did not want to put her or his sisters in any more danger.

"Mukhs will drive you to the airport. The driver had been given leave while we were away and is still not back from his village."

Mukhs showed up just then and gave his friend a concerned look. "Listen, *yaar*. We are trying to get to the bottom of this, but you need to get back to the US. Those guys who were here mean business. We can't afford to fool around. Something really strange is going on. It has something to do with you and your work at the university."

Sahil was taken aback. "What the hell does that even mean, Mukhs? Tell me exactly what they said. And who is 'they' anyway?"

Mukhs just grabbed the suitcase and backpack and threw it in the back of his jeep. "Look, just get in. We can talk on the way to the airport."

No matter what Mukhs told him—the scenario of the raid, the Taliban or extremists who attacked Abdul Nagr, his work at the university—nothing was coming to any reasonable conclusion. The worst was that he didn't understand why he had to leave the country with such urgency.

Nothing could have prepared him for the reception waiting for him at the airport. There were security guards, police, and agency types in suits there as he started toward his gate, ready to board. They accosted him and put him in a holding room where they questioned him for what seemed like several hours.

"I have missed my flight, sir. I must see if there are any other seats available," he pleaded with the authorities, but they were not bothered by that in the least. The questioning was sporadic and fragmented. His laptop and backpack were strewn on the table, and he was tied down in a small wooden chair. He tried to explain what he was doing in Pakistan, and at one point, someone he knew—the cousin that his mother had mentioned—came by and peeked through the glass door, looking apologetic but obviously powerless in this arena. How and when he arrived at the prison-type facility here and now was a mystery to him. The last thing he remembered was asking for some water and the officer giving him a hard slap on his face.

* * * * *

He finally made enough noise, one last attempt. He thought, *I have to do this and get the hell out of this place!*

"I demand to see a supervisor," he yelled. "Get me someone *now*!"

The burly guard gave him another angry look and loudly began spewing insults at him and shouted that he would probably die here before seeing anything close to a supervisor.

At this point, Sahil was ready to take the torture just to shift himself from this stagnant environment that gave no inkling of hope whatsoever.

Just then, a more sharply dressed man in a clean white uniform came up to the cell and took the guard by the arm. "What is the issue here, and why are you screaming? Didn't we talk about this in our training?"

The guard immediately straightened up and saluted the uniformed man. "Sorry, sir. This prisoner has been making trouble ever since he got here several months ago. He is refusing to give us the information that we need. We should really put him with the waterboarding group."

The uniformed man looked at the guard, showing signs of contempt on his otherwise smooth and pleasant face. "Oh, really? Now you are making decisions for the senior commanders here, eh?"

The guard seemed to redden and shrink a bit at the remark as Sahil looked on. He realized that now was his chance to intervene and make his case. "Please, sir, I must appeal to you. I have no idea why I am being held here and am sure there was some mistake. There are people in Islamabad who you can contact and verify my innocence. Just please give me a chance to speak to you for five minutes."

The commander slowly turned his attention to Sahil, looking him up and down, taking in the tattered and filthy state of his clothing. And then he looked directly into his eyes. Sahil could sense that this man was used to wielding power and probably making life-and-death decisions for many lucky or unlucky souls.

Something shifted in his gaze from steely control to a quiet flow, and the man's eyes turned a soft shade with a golden glow. Something happened between them, and Sahil could not explain it, but he felt a hand on his head and heard a voice whisper in his ear, "It will be okay, my boy. Just be patient."

No one else was in the cell with him, and the voice was clear. Sahil did not waver in his stance, but he stood there, just staring back at the commander. He held that gaze for longer than Sahil understood, and then he then turned to the guard. "Let him wash up. Get him some clean clothes and bring him to my office. And there will be no more yelling. Is that understood?"

Sahil could feel the tightness from his spine relax, and his breath came out slow and steady. The guard was more irritated than ever, and he shot a venomous look of disdain at Sahil before unlocking the cell and grabbing his arm to lead him to the cavernous area with pipes coming out of the stone walls. These were meant for showering or washing up, as was done to the prisoners once a month.

The guard told him to strip and yelled at another guard to stay and keep watch on him while he fetched a clean jumpsuit. As dirty and dingy as this place was, just having even a cold stream of water and a small bar of soap that he found swirling on the ground there was enough to lift Sahil's spirits. And he prayed that something came of this that would get him out of here.

He had woken up early this morning as he could hear the shouts of the guards along with the clamor of iron gates opening and closing to let in more prisoners. He knelt down and felt the thin beam of light from the measly skylight above him as he closed his eyes and prayed for those prisoners to be shown justice and humanity. But if they had fallen to the wrong call of killers and evildoers, then God help them. He prayed for his family and for his own safe release, and then he prayed for Zaina. How many prayers get answered, and how many get lost or put to the end of the list? he wondered.

He quickly dried himself with the shred of a towel handed to him and got dressed. He ignored both the guards who were standing there, eyeing him with nefarious looks and laughing as he hastily finished dressing. His handcuffs were locked back on, and he was led down a dark corridor, which turned a corner and led to a large black door.

The guard unlocked the door, and this took them out to a wide courtyard. Sahil shielded his eyes from the sun, not used to the bright light of day. They walked for a few minutes toward a redbrick building and to a set of glass-enclosed offices, one of which led to a room where the commander was seated.

He motioned for Sahil to sit down and asked the guard to take off his handcuffs. He began to ask some questions. "So what were you doing in the northern areas, Mr. Khan? Our records indicate that you flew from the US and came to Islamabad then went into the Swat Valley, where we are tracking the Taliban and Al-Qaeda militants and terrorist cells."

So they did have his information and knew his background. Sahil did not understand what the issue was. "Yes, sir. Of course. I am a doctorate student and had finished my semester and was on holiday with my family. We often go to the Swat Valley during the summer when I visit them in Islamabad. I am not sure what happened and why this is presenting a problem."

The commander looked at Sahil carefully. "Can you tell me exactly what happened that day that the Taliban came into the compound of Abdul Nagr and raided and cleared out everyone—everyone but you? How did you escape that raid? What type of work were you doing for them? You are a nuclear scientist, are you not?"

Sahil was stunned that there was any connection between his work at the university and this whole mess with the raid, ending up with him in some godforsaken prison in who knows where. "First of all, sir, I would like to clear up the fact that I have nothing to do with any terrorist activity or cell. My work at the university is strictly academic and for teaching purposes to my engineering students and to complete my thesis. I have never shared or intend to share scientific data with any such groups, if that is what you are implying."

He continued, "I was on holiday, as I mentioned. My friend and I were having…a picnic in one of the caves when the raid occurred. I heard the gunshots, and because I understand Pashto, I knew that they were looking for American spies that had been turning them in to the government. We hid in the cave until it was safe to come out the next morning. It was very traumatic and difficult to get back to Islamabad safely. You can speak to my friend and her family to corroborate my statement."

The officer looked at Sahil, carefully assessing the account of what he had just heard. "Ah, and who is this friend that you mention? What is his name?"

"Oh, it is a she, sir. Her name is Zaina."

The commander's eyebrows lifted slightly, and Sahil was sure he saw a slight upturn in his smile as he continued, "Does the young lady have a last name, family name, or any address where we can locate her?"

This was where Sahil was at a loss. How is it that one can spend two weeks with someone, get completely enthralled by their every word and movement, and yet not even get a full name or contact information.

His head fell forward, and he simply shook it back and forth. "There was no time. By the time we got to Islamabad, her family had come to get her. And we had never met before, so I didn't have any contact information for her."

"I see. So you are saying that the only witness for your innocence is this girl whom you have never met before you got to Swat and have never seen since. Is that right?"

Sahil was quiet. He sounded like a complete moron and probably very guilty of the actual accusations that were being held against him.

"We have strong reason to believe—from a source at the university—that you were providing nuclear and scientific information to the Taliban, and that you are the one who arranged that raid to ward off any spies that would reveal your identity."

Sahil straightened up, and his eyes were incredulous. "Sir, that could not be farther from the truth. Can you give me the name of the person or persons that would provide you such wrong information? I will call them right now and clear this whole mess up!"

The commander shifted in his seat and crossed his arms. "That is not so easy, young man. You see, we have our sources placed there for that exact reason—to keep an eye on these sorts of activities. And the person you were dealing with found out about your direction and communications with Islamabad."

Sahil drew a long breath. This was going nowhere very quickly, and he had to put a stop to it. He racked his brain as to who could possibly turn him in like this and why. When he was detained at the airport, they took away all his papers and his passport, cell phone, and laptop, which had his work on it. But that was his dissertation, which was almost completed. His paper was titled "The Global Effects of Nuclear Warfare." It was completely theoretical but based on research he had been doing in the South Asian region for a while. He could imagine that if it had gotten into the wrong hands, it presented a dangerous and lethal outcome. But again, it was just his thesis, and it did not have anything to do with what they were accusing him of. The calls and communication with his family to Islamabad were all personal and had nothing to do with nuclear or scientific information. Something was missing. Something was wrong.

"Can you tell me, Mr. Khan? Are you loyal to the United States or to the Taliban?"

There was a silence as Sahil tried to process the absurd accusation. He stood up finally, and as sincerely as he could, he answered the question. This was becoming dangerously real, and he had a tiny beam of light: the truth that he needed to impart to this man.

"Sir, that is such a question that I am shocked to have to answer. I am a student at a prestigious university in the United States. I find myself very fortunate to be in that position and to use my knowledge to teach and inspire other students to further their knowledge. That is my goal. I have never had nor have any inclination toward terrorist groups such as the Taliban. In fact, I detest such ideologies as they are in direct conflict with the teachings of Islam. There is no glory in killing or being killed, as they preach.

"I am a follower of a peaceful ideology, such as Sufism, which is why the Taliban attacked that compound. They are extremists and destroy anyone that espouses inclusiveness and tolerance. In fact, Tajuddin Baba came from India. He was the one who influenced another enlightened sheikh, Abdul Baba, who guided my good friend's uncle to establish that retreat in the Swat Valley. I have no idea why I was targeted, and you can talk to a number of professors at the university to confirm this. Someone has given you wrong information. I am innocent and do not belong here."

The words just flowed out of him like water from a spring. He was not even sure if it was his own voice since he was beginning to doubt himself as the questioning became more intense.

The commander quickly interjected, "We have tried to contact the professors whose names you have given us and had worked with you, and none of them are available. They have left the university." And then, for reasons Sahil could not fathom, he suddenly stopped talking and stared at Sahil with such intensity that Sahil felt his spine begin to tingle.

Abruptly, without any hesitation, the commander stood and held his hand up. "Wait. Hold on, hold on. What do you know about Tajuddin Baba?"

Sahil hesitated. He remembered reading much about him when he was trying to understand the history of Abdul Nagr, and in fact, the library there had quite a few publications. He also spent a few sessions with Babajan, having lengthy discussions on the subject. There was a direct line of succession with this humble saint that Babajan had and had been connected with and through several generations of guidance and thought.

"Well, I know that he was a great Sufi saint and that he is buried in Nagpur, India, and that he has created a worldwide following because of his nonviolent and benevolent spiritual messages and writings."

The commander looked at Sahil as if witnessing a ghost, and what happened next was quite surreal and extraordinary. He walked slowly up to Sahil and lightly touched his forehead, his eyes suddenly emanating that same eerie golden glow as earlier. There were tears in his eyes, and he pulled Sahil toward him in a gentle embrace. "I am so sorry, my son. Every challenge is a test. Please forgive me." He then called in the guard standing at the door and asked him to bring all of Sahil's papers and a release form.

Within one hour, the papers were shuffled and signed, and Sahil's original clothes, documents, phone, and laptop were returned to him. He was told to wait until his ride to the airport arrived.

When he asked the driver what the commander's name was, as he would like to thank him for his help, the driver just looked at him in an odd way. "No commanders on this post, sir. Only guards."

He was driven, with a blindfold on, to another area. When the jeep arrived, the blindfold was removed. The place looked vaguely familiar. He was then transferred to a car, which took him to the Islamabad airport.

His family and friends were waiting there for him. There were strict instructions for him to fly directly back to the States and not to stay in Islamabad for more than eight hours. He was greeted with tears. He felt so relieved to see his mother and sisters and their shocked faces at his appearance that he physically broke down. His exhaustion and stress from the last grueling months had weathered him, and it showed on his unshaven face and gaunt physique.

"Oh, my darling. What have they done to you? I need to take you home so you can rest and eat something." His mother cried.

His sisters echoed that sentiment and wrapped themselves around him protectively.

"No, Ammi. I must take this next flight back to the US. I have strict instructions. I was very lucky to get out of that detention place. I really don't know how my release happened. It was like a miracle. I can't take any more chances. I will be finc."

Zaina

BOSTON (2016)

As she finished up her reading and note-taking, she closed the heavy volume of *Art and Antiquities in the Eighteenth Century*. Zaina looked around at the graduate library. All was quiet; a low hum of the humidifiers could be heard as high shelves of books towered around her. The emerald green of the low glass lamps reminded her of those large bees in the summertime with their blue-green bulb of a torso. These low lamps sent a cool stream of greenish light throughout the large hall.

She lay her head on the table, exhausted and wiped out from trying to piece together the mystery of her lost love. It's been over a year and still no word or sign of Sahil anywhere. She took out a blank sheet of paper and started writing, not sure where it was coming from, but it just had to come out. She had no other outlet to express this love.

> You came and I awoke
> Light into Day
> A Babe in Arms
> Searching the Way
> The Flowers turned their heads
> Mistaking you for the Sun
> None of this surprised me
> I knew you were the One
> Now a mere mist
> A warm refrain
> A Fallen scarf in the summer rain
> Oh, ethereal breath in the night
> It is you I search for
> When looking for the Light
> Alas, it is said
> Better to have Loved and Lost

So let it be then
That I have loved
And forever I am lost

She then took out her small tasbih, the string of tiger's-eye prayer beads that she kept close. She wore it as a bracelet sometimes but mostly kept it as a lucky charm when taking an exam or going on a journey. She gently rolled her finger over each bead, whispering a small prayer for each one until the end. As she lay her head there doing this, her eyes became heavy with sleep, and she dozed off. A tap on her shoulder woke her, and she quickly sat up, startled by the stranger in front of her.

"Hi. Sorry to bother you. Do you have a minute? My name is Nora, and I worked in the engineering department when Sahil was there."

Zaina regained her composure and looked carefully at the young woman in front of her, a frail brunette with large spectacles. Zaina was intrigued and motioned to her. "Oh, please sit down. Can we talk for a few minutes?"

Nora looked around suspiciously. "I think it would be best if we go somewhere off campus."

At this point, Zaina was desperate for any information, so she agreed as the young woman helped her collect her books. They began walking toward the exit of the library.

"I have a car," Nora said. "There's a small coffee shop on the other side of the campus where they don't have much of a menu, so it's not really popular. That may be better."

Zaina's instincts were battling to resist, so she had to question the woman. "Can I ask why all the secrecy, Nora? I have a lot of work to do and not much time. I really don't want to be driving all over the place."

Lately, it seemed to Zaina that her luck was running dry, and it was partly due to exhaustive failures to find Sahil. She now was so desperate as to follow this strange person and even get into their car—an action that would have shocked her pre-Sahil self.

As they got outdoors, the young woman turned to Zaina and looked at her very directly. "You should know that who you are looking for has been set up and framed so others can take over the department. It's not something that we can just chat about. It's pretty serious."

Zaina just followed Nora to her car and slipped in quietly. They drove for about ten minutes and pulled up to what looked like a coffee shop in a strip mall. They made their way in and were seated face-to-face in one of the booths toward the back, which Nora chose. She took a deep breath. "Okay. So I was there when you were asking around for Sahil Khan. Dr. Kimberly Branson was his TA. She knows him very well."

Zaina was trying to wrap her head around this new information, one that completely put her approach as to whom to trust in a tailspin. "I'm sorry, but can I ask who you are and what your connection is to all this? How did you know Sahil, and where did you get this information? Can I see some ID? Right now, I am finding it hard to trust my own instincts, much less a total stranger. I hope you understand."

Nora nodded. "I understand. I was hired as a TA for Dr. Branson," she said. She shuffled through a sandy-colored suede satchel and pulled out a weathered brown wallet. "Here is my card. The address is now different, but my contact info and all is the same."

Zaina took the card and read it:

> Dr. Nora Cumberland
> Associate Professor, College of Engineering
> Mentor, Advisor

She seemed very young to be an associate professor. Academics was known to age people, in Zaina's experience.

"I am no longer with the university but had come to collect my things when I saw you with Dr. Branson, and I heard what she was telling you. I had to follow you and fill you in. It is very wrong what is going on there," she continued, her voice both urgent and breathless. "I was there after Sahil Khan left for Pakistan. Within a few weeks, he was put on a watch list—a terrorist watch list.

And we were told not to tell anyone that he had any position here or anything to do with the university. In fact, all the professors, aside from Dr. Branson, were given double-paying jobs in other states and countries to leave the department, and Dr. Branson hired a whole new teaching staff."

Zaina slumped back into the booth and shut her eyes. This was more than she could expect to handle with on her own. But at the same time, she had to be careful not to involve anyone that was not completely trustworthy. "Nora…Dr. Cumberland, I truly appreciate your information and you taking the risk to tell me, but I am at a loss as to where to begin to resolve the issue of how to find him. Do you know where he could be?"

"He was taken and put in a holding cell for accused terrorists, either in Pakistan or somewhere offshore."

Zaina gasped at this new information. "My god. Are you certain about this? Do you think he could have been tortured or worse? I don't know if he is even still alive. Why on earth would they do this to him?" She felt like someone had punched her in the stomach and left an ache that she had never experienced before. And now Zaina's voice had reached a fever pitch, reaching a point where she was trembling, and tears began to well in her eyes.

Nora immediately held her hand and took her chin in the other. "Look, Zaina. You will have to be strong and strategic. Something is not right. It's going on in that department, and you have the key."

Zaina looked at her, gathering some courage with those words. "What key? What should I do? What *can* I do?" she asked.

"You see, I am not supposed to be here. I moved across two states but needed some things that I had left behind. It was just luck that I happened to be in the hall when you were talking to Dr. Branson, and she did not see me. You have my cell number. I must go. They made it very clear that we need to be out of the university area by a certain timeline. Start with Dr. Branson. She is the center of what happened. She knew and worked with Sahil very closely. She knew about his friends, his family, and his ties to his country.

Where and when the wall fell, I don't know. I just know that there was a whole team effort to get him out."

"Okay, okay. I am starting to understand somewhat." Zaina took a deep breath and exhaled. Just having this weird puzzle piece in her hand was a strong start, and she didn't want to drop it now. "I really do appreciate this, and I will be calling you as I figure things out. I just don't know if I can do it alone."

They started to get up when the waitress came and asked what they wanted to order. Nora addressed the waitress, "Nothing for me, thanks. I have to leave. Will you be able to get back to campus okay, Zaina?"

"Sure, no worries. I will take an Uber back. I just need a few minutes here to get my head clear. A coffee and a tuna wrap please," she offered to the waitress, who took the order and walked off. She just realized that she hadn't eaten all day, and it was already after two. She would need her strength to figure out this mess, and this anxiety and lightheadedness would not get better by starving.

As Nora was getting ready to leave, she held Zaina's hand and whispered in her ear, "You are not alone."

Zaina felt a tremor in her hand as Nora released it and gave her a warm smile. "Take care, Zaina," Nora said as she left the coffee shop.

While waiting for her coffee and sandwich, Zaina turned over the card that Nora had given her and saw something scribbled in pencil on the back. There were two notes. One looked like "refuge@mountainsaints.com." The other was a code or maybe a password of some sort: "pact911nf."

What an odd couple of notes to have on a calling card, she thought. Without hesitation, she pulled out her laptop and first put in a search for the URL site. It was a link to Abdul Nagr, the estate up in the mountains that belonged to her uncle. Zaina couldn't believe her eyes. There was a committee or board of some familiar faces under "Meet Our Leaders" along with a few she had never seen.

She continued to search and found more links to other saints and their places of gathering. There was a Qadr Baba, a Baba Mohiuddin, and then a Tajuddin Baba in India. What did all this mean, and how did Nora fit into this? Zaina's head was beginning to spin. She would need to go back and do some more research and figure this out.

Just then, the waitress came with her coffee and sandwich.

"Oh, thanks. I think I will have to take it to go. How much do I owe you?"

The waitress just smiled. "Hey, no worries. It was taken care of! I'll get you a container and a to-go cup."

Zaina was surprised to hear this. She didn't remember Nora stopping to pay the waitress or anything on her way out. In fact, she seemed to be in a rush to get out of there. *Things are getting weirder and weirder*, she thought as she pulled up her Uber app and ordered a car.

The next morning, after a restless night and then attending morning class, Zaina came back to her apartment and set up her laptop.

She tried to search for terrorist prisons in and around Islamabad, then in Pakistan, and then in the US. Except for human rights organizations calling for action to prevent violations, she was not getting any specific locations or information. She should have known better. The DHS and CIA were not going to divulge this type of location to just public view; it could become a security issue. She supposed she had to think smarter.

The rest of the day went quickly as she finished up a paper and grabbed a quick bite at the local coffee shop. It wasn't until she was rummaging through her purse for change that she noticed Nora's card in the side pocket.

Wait, she thought. *What about that weird code?* She hadn't even looked into that at all: "pact911nf." She decided to give Nora a call. She had to get some answers.

She dialed the number and waited. The phone rang for about four rings, and then an automated voice came on. "The number you have dialed is no longer in service. Please check your number and dial again."

You have got to be shitting me. What is this? And what is happening! Her head and focus were going in a tailspin again.

Zaina was almost ready to bang her head on her desk at this point. She was going nowhere fast. She held the card in her hand and stared at the code. She traced her steps back to the day she went to the Engineering Department building and tried to remember exactly what had happened with Dr. Branson. Nora mentioned something about her having a key. That receptionist was no help either, but she did mention needing special access to get into the administration and office areas of the higher-level departments.

Zaina quickly grabbed her phone. She slung her cross-body bag across her chest and began a brisk stride toward the Engineering Building. Whatever answers she needed to find Sahil and get to the bottom of this lay in that building where he worked and was an integral part of.

It was well after seven in the evening by now, and dusk had started to fall on campus. She knew she should be careful not to roam around alone after dark as there had been some cases of attacks in and around the area. But Zaina was determined, and no such dark fears were going to stop her now.

She said a quick prayer and wrapped her prayer beads around her wrist as she made way to the front of the building. The building was dark and unusually quiet. The front and main doors were locked, so she began walking around to the side entrance where she had seen some people coming out of last time. There was a stretch of woods just adjacent to the back of the building, and she thought that she heard some kind of rustling.

Probably squirrels or birds flitting about, she thought to herself. She had read about modern humankind being insulated through modern technology and urban life so as to suppress the inner instincts of self-preservation that animals have in the natural world. That early man could survive because his instincts for survival were heightened by predators and the like. She felt that modern man had to develop other types of survival skills, like earning a living and keeping healthy to survive now. But it was true. She would never be able to survive in the jungle or woods on her own.

"Hey, do you have a light?"

The man came up from behind her. He did not seem like a student. He had on a worn-down army-green field jacket and a rough beard. His eyes were glassy as he looked her over, and he smelled like stale bread.

"Um, hi! No…so sorry. No lighter."

She realized that she was somewhat stammering but tried to stay friendly, as if on cue from her previous thoughts. Her instincts were now on alert.

"Oh, no worries, babe. I was going to chill out here, but we can find something else to do." He came closer and began to put his arm around her waist.

"Uh…jeez. That would be great, but my boyfriend is waiting for me, so I really have to go!" She moved away slowly but deliberately and tried to move his hand off her waist, but he grabbed her hand and twisted it behind her back while shoving his body onto hers, his watery eyes glazing into her. Her stomach felt queasy as his stench wafted into her nostrils and the stark reality of what he was about to attempt came to her. She could not vomit now, no matter what.

"Stop!" she screamed as loud as she could even though she knew no one was around to help her. She then kicked up her knee into his torso, shoving it harder than she knew she could. He buckled over with a grunt and flailed his arms about. She assumed he was already high or drunk, so his balance was inevitably questionable, but she couldn't count on that.

She ran back to her car before he could look up, and she got in, locking the doors as fast as possible. She dialed the campus police and reported the incident along with a description of the jerk. She was shaking and took a sip from her water bottle before driving farther out to a well-lit parking lot. She found a spot near the main building where she could still get a view of the area where she was attacked. She waited there until the campus police came and found the man keeled over in the woods. He was throwing up.

She watched as they took him away, and they called her to come and identify him so they could do an arrest. She asked if they could do a video call because she was already very traumatized. She was relieved that they agreed and thanked her for her help. She was also asked if she needed any kind of medical treatment.

"No thanks. I'm okay. I was able to get away before he could do any real harm, thank God."

Zaina went back to her apartment; she didn't have the energy to complete the task she had gone to the Engineering building for. It seemed that every turn presented a blockade that made her more and more hopeless. She knew though, that she hadn't come this far to stop now. If she didn't follow through this task tonight, she would not be able to go there for a few days. She had exams coming up, and the university would be shutting down for winter break.

She took a hot shower then changed into some warm leggings and a bulky sweatshirt. She tied her hair in a bun and put on the Detroit Lions beanie that her cousin had given her as a token because she got into Michigan State but chose not to go there. Her black down jacket should keep her warm enough.

She made a coffee and drank it in the car. It was around nine thirty in the evening now, and things should be quieter on campus. She put a Taser and mace spray in the pockets of her coat. She also kept her phone flashlight ready as she parked and walked to check on the front of the Engineering building again. She was starting to tremble but checked herself. *This is ridiculous. It can't happen twice, you dummy. Besides that, you are well prepared. Let's do this!*

Sahil's words echoed in her head for when they had to head back from the incident in Swat. Was she channeling him? Maybe. He gave her courage—that she knew for sure.

She checked the front entrance again: still locked. *Obviously.* So she walked around to the back of the building, one eye on the ominous woods looming in the background. She found a large metal door and a stairwell going to what must be the basement. The door was heavy and looked like something you would see in a bank's vault area. She wasn't sure what to do but remembered that she had that Nora woman's card in her coat pocket.

She pulled out the crushed card. There was a keypad on the door, and Zaina instinctively punched in the code from the back of Nora's card, "pact911nf," adding a hashtag at the end.

Suddenly, a green light flickered, and the door clicked open. She let out a huge sigh of relief. She had no idea what she was looking for, but this was a good sign. As she padded toward the reception area, she was afraid that "Red" would be there and recognize her. Luckily, the area was deserted, and she could get past that and move toward the corridors marked Administration and Offices.

There were several clear glass-enclosed cubicles with computers and papers scattered about on the desks. These rows of offices led to a redbrick walled hallway where the doors were more solid, save for a few doors that had a narrow rectangular window in the center.

Zaina peeked in a few of them to see empty desks, and when she turned the knobs, they were locked. The nameplates on the doors were blank, almost as if they had been wiped out.

As she approached the last door, she peeked into the narrow glass window of the door and saw Dr. Branson laughing and talking with what was probably another professor. He was tall. He wore jeans and a black T-shirt and had a beard that only went across his lower face, not mustache or upper lip. Zaina had some recollection that the extreme factions of certain Taliban men would have these types of beards. They were standing very close to each other, and at some point, he put his arms around her, and they locked in an embrace.

Zaina quickly stepped to the side so they wouldn't see her and put her ear to the door. She heard both Dr. Branson and this man talking in Pashto. The woman was speaking in Pashto!

As Zaina listened, she did not understand the language. Then it occurred to her that the man looked vaguely familiar. *Think, think,* she pressed her memory. She then realized he looked like one of the board members that she had seen on the mountain saints website. What was she supposed to do now? This was much deeper than she could have imagined, and she was starting to feel very nervous about being here.

She slowly crept away from the door, hoping to slip away and go back to her apartment. Confronting Dr. Branson now was not an option, not without some more information.

Just then, she heard the door jerk open, and both Dr. Branson and the bearded man were staring at her in astonishment. "Zaina, what the hell are you doing here? And how did you get into the building?" Her voice was stern and cold, not the same as when she had talked to her just days before.

"Er, um, th-that redheaded girl let me through. I told her I was looking for you," she stammered as Dr. Branson's clear blue eyes pierced through her lies.

"Don't lie to me. She is not at the desk. No one is here. They leave at five, and only the professors and admin have access to this building."

By this time, Zaina was beginning to lose her nerves. But she pushed on, her voice strong and defiant. "How do you know Pashto? And what do you have to do with Sahil's disappearance, Dr. Branson?"

There was a deafening silence as she passed a look to the bearded guy.

"I have no idea where you are getting your ideas or questions from, but you are in way over your head!" She then grabbed Zaina's arm and brought her face close so that Zaina could see the irises of her eyes. They were like polar ice caps, getting ready to burst into an avalanche.

"Kim, let her go. She is just concerned about her boyfriend," the bearded man stated softly. He then smiled and looked at Zaina with a pathetic gaze.

"Majid, don't interfere. This one is a troublemaker. I know her type," she shot back at him.

"He is not my—" Zaina started to protest.

But Dr. Branson would not let go and said in a growl, with her teeth clenched, "You are way out of your league here. And if you know what's good for you, missy, you will pack up your stuff and choose another university to dabble in your art theories."

As she listened to this threat, it dawned on Zaina that she never mentioned that she was in the Art Department here at the university. How did this woman get that information? She had most likely been doing background checks on her as well. "Let go of my arm. You are hurting me!" Zaina yelled as she tried to yank her arm free.

Before she could wrestle away from Dr. Branson's grip, Zaina heard a loud shuffling down the other end of the corridor. As she looked up, she saw something that she could not have imagined in her wildest dreams. It was Sahil—or at least a scaled-down version of him, gaunter and leaner than she remembered—marching down the hall with at least half a dozen uniformed officers and a gentleman in a dark suit and tie.

"Kim, let go of her. Now!" shouted Sahil.

The other officers were coming forward when the man in the suit shouted in a commanding voice, "Dr. Kimberly Branson! Dr. Majid Hameed! Freeze! CIA! You are both under arrest for treason against the United States. You have the right to remain silent—"

Before he could continue with the Miranda rights, Majid reached behind and pulled out a revolver. The uniformed officers swiftly began locking and loading their guns, and you could see a SWAT team rushing in and assembling their weapons behind them, but it was too late. He was so quick, and he pointed the gun at his head. There was a loud bang as the shot echoed, booming through the halls.

At this point, Zaina screamed and ran to Sahil, who held her tight as Dr. Branson fell on Majid's collapsed and bloodied corpse. A long guttural cry of "No, no, no! Majid, why?" escaped from her terrified face. She looked at Sahil, pointing a finger at him. "You. You caused this!"

There was blood splattered everywhere, and Zaina trembled in Sahil's arms as she could not wipe out the image of the bearded man's face exploding right in front of her.

There was a lot of noise as the EMT team came through, and ambulance sirens blared in full roar. The officers and the SWAT team asked them all to freeze as they assessed the damage and put handcuffs on a struggling and grief-stricken Dr. Kimberly Branson.

Sahil ignored Kim's accusations and motioned to the man in the suit, who nodded and came over to shake his hand. "Thank you, Mr. Khan, for your cooperation. We could not have done this without you. We have been tracking this operation for years, and it has been a nightmare to pin down."

"Most welcome. I am relieved that it is over. Now, if you don't mind, I think I will be taking this young lady home to get some much-needed rest," he said as he looked down into Zaina's face.

She was still shattered and confused. There were small droplets of blood on her cheeks from the suicide of Majid Hameed.

"Of course, you both are free to go. I may be calling you and the young lady for further details later. Let me take care of this mess right now though. I will arrange for a squad car to take you wherever you need to go." He spoke with a determined sense of purpose, and Zaina could tell he was one that all the other men in the room would rely on and trust to bring this horrible chapter to a close.

They made it back to Zaina's place in an unmarked police car as Sahil did not think it wise to walk around campus with blood-splattered faces, she was too exhausted from the fatal encounter to argue or make any decisions at this point.

When they got to her apartment, everything appeared to look the same, but in fact, nothing was the same. She turned to him, eyes wide with worry, and started posing the questions that were circling in her mind. "Sahil, where have you been? What happened just now? Why did Dr. Branson accuse you and of what?"

There was a pause, and he just looked at her with that same softness in his eyes that she remembered from when they first met. "Let's just take it one step at a time, Zaina. I will tell you everything. But first, it might be a good idea to wash up and change. Are you hungry?"

She just kept staring at him, as if in a dream. "Famished," she almost whispered.

He smiled. "I am going to order some Thai food for us, and then we will talk. Does that sound okay?"

There could be no sweeter words for Zaina to hear at this time. She was reminded of Sahil's cool composure at the time of their escape together. *Was that actually over a year ago?*

She took a deep breath. "Better than okay, Sahil. It's perfect."

As they sat at her small round dining table in the kitchen, emptying cartons of drunken noodles and chicken pad thai on their plates, Sahil started from the beginning. "Kimberly apparently had been working with the CIA to expose any terrorist activity in our department. Unbeknownst to me, there were factions of Taliban that had integrated into top American universities, funded by Saudi extremist groups to gather intelligence on nuclear bombs and destructive devices, even smuggling uranium to the terrorist cells. I later realized why she was so keen on getting to know me better. I mistakenly thought it was for my good looks!"

He laughed, and Zaina laughed with him. It was so good to laugh again, and his humor in the face of all this adversity was what reminded her why she loved him so much, and now she was certain of this fact.

"Go on," she said, smiling.

"Well, turns out that our clever Dr. Branson had bigger plans than the CIA was aware of. And when she started suspecting this Dr. Majid fellow, he romanced her and offered her millions of dollars in compensation if she would cover for him. She not only covered for him but she basically got sucked into their organization and was working both sides. At least, that is what it seemed like. The government was able to trace over five million dollars in hidden bank accounts back to her. In fact, from the recordings we have heard, Majid had promised her a foolproof escape route for the both of them to marry and spend their lives together. He was on the board of trustees for Abdul Nagr, posing as a Sufi supporter but working against them and with the extremist groups all along.

"It was only when he got admitted to the university for his PhD that he met Kim and realized what she was doing. Who knows if his plans were real or if he was just taking her for a ride? I had seen him here and there in the department and asked her a few times if she knew him, which she denied. I told her that he seemed a bit dodgy to me, and maybe we should try to report him to the authorities. I think they suspected that I was getting too close to finding out their movements and intentions. I became a perfect scapegoat."

Zaina took a deep breath and tried to take in and process all the layers of this operation and how both she and Sahil were reeled into it. "I don't know what to say. That is incredible. You know, I did notice a gold necklace she wore with her name in Arabic calligraphy, and Majid's face looked so familiar from the website for Abdul Nagr, but I would never have thought much of it until now. But seriously, tell me. What did all this have to do with you?"

"Yes," he continued, "that is the scary part. When I told Kim that I wanted to go to Pakistan to see my family, she was very keen on helping me wrap up and cover for me if needed. Of course, why would I have any reason to suspect her? She was an excellent TA and knew the courses well. Besides, it was the summer semester, so she only had to oversee two courses. I did get the feeling that she wanted more from me. I underestimated her.

"She needed a decoy to turn over to the CIA and US government so it would look like she was doing her job. She had her contacts in Islamabad, through Majid, to trace my location. And together, they masterminded the raid in Swat, hoping to trap me and turn me over right there. The CIA informants didn't know that we had hidden in that cave. But when they found me at the airport, it was even more plausible that I was part of the terrorist group since I was not captured. With me out of the way, Kim and Majid could continue to supply information to the terrorist group and collect money from them."

Zaina just looked at Sahil's face. The gentle way in which he was explaining it all made her heart hurt. After over a year in a rotting jail cell, his face was withdrawn, and there were dark circles under his eyes. There was no anger or pain, just a sense of relief and gratitude.

"I cannot imagine what you must have gone through in that jail cell, Sahil." She instinctively placed her hand on his. "But I am so glad you managed to get out, and I cannot believe you are here with me now. You have no idea how frantic I had been trying to locate you! How did they finally release you and get to the bottom of all this?"

"Zaina, I had no way of contacting you or my family and friends. You will not believe this, but it's a really strange thing that happened. I was shouting and making noise, like I did every day, to speak to a superior to state my case. So finally, one day, and this particular morning, I kept praying and thinking of light—of *Noor* to guide me and give me strength—because a new group of prisoners was getting checked in. And I was praying for them too.

"I was thinking, getting some answers in a way, that there are many trials in life, and this is just another one that I must get through. I never wavered in my faith, though I was wearing down physically. I swear there were days when I said to myself, 'This is it. I give up.' It was so unbearable. Then I thought of you. And then it was Babajan's premonition to me, his warning, that kept ringing in my head. To stay strong and be patient. Also, he said something very specific about my difficult time that only made sense to me now. That the person who is in charge is not your enemy, that every difficulty in life is a test. How and why those words came to me then, I do not know. I just used every ounce of determination I had left to push through. So…"

He paused to take a sip of water.

"Sahil, it's okay. We can talk about this later. You need to rest." She was getting the feeling that with everything coming to a head, his eyes were beginning to haze with exhaustion.

"No, no. It's okay. I want to tell you everything. So this new officer, whom I have never seen, comes and orders the guards to let me clean up and come to his office. He questions me, but in a very decent way, not like the other Neanderthals at the prison. He was patient and kind. It was such a relief to talk to someone who would listen and try to understand my situation. I tell him my story, profess my innocence, and he just looked at me in the strangest way.

"We talked for a while, and when I mentioned about Babajan and other pirs, he just stared at me. I thought maybe he didn't believe me and was going to throw me back into the cell, but he kept asking me more about the connection I had to your uncle. Then, after about an hour of this, he called in the other guy, told him to start the release process to let me go, and he was gone. It was the most bizarre thing that

I had ever witnessed! The rest all fell into place when we I got back and helped the authorities start digging into Kim's role in the operation."

Zaina understood exactly what had happened, which was the same type of feeling she got from Nora. Wait…Nora. *Noor* meaning "divine light." She told him of her encounter with the woman in the library, but he had no recollection of such a name.

She knew this conversation was beginning to weigh heavily on him but needed to ask him about one more missing piece. "Can I ask you if you know the meaning of the code to enter the building that was given to me? It was *pact911nf*."

His eyes widened, and he nodded. "Sure. I created it for myself. It stands for 'Patriot Act, 9/11, Never Forget.' But how did you know my code? No one else has it. We have each chosen our own passwords."

Zaina just smiled. "You really don't want to know that. Some small miracles are just that."

There was no way to explain it, and she didn't really want to. Some things are just a matter of mind and heart over matter.

A small prayer of gratitude escaped her lips, and she felt an inner peace that she had lost somewhere along the way. Someone was looking out for them; this she knew for sure. What the future holds for her and Sahil remains to be seen, but for now, she was drunk on drunken noodles, and the only person in the world whom she wished to be with was here with her. Amen to that.

"Oh, and one more thing." He looked at her with that familiar sparkle in his eyes. "Can I get your cell phone number and email please?"

Epilogue

SWAT VALLEY, THE SUMMER OF 2015

They climbed to the top of the clearing, where an unobstructed view of the mountains and valley was visible for miles. It had been a perfect day to escape from all the frenzy of activity at the main house as preparations were underway for a special guest who was coming to see her uncle. The three-and-a-half-mile hike was exhilarating, but now it was time to take a break.

"Here." Sahil motioned to a large flat rock jutting over the thistle and brush. He pulled off his backpack and took out the water bottles and two small apples that he had hurriedly collected from the kitchen. Hoori had shot a questioning look at him, but then she knew more than she let on and laughed as she added some nuts and dates to the bag.

They both crouched slowly and then sat on the comfortable makeshift platform overlooking the immense beauty of the valley. It was still early, so a pink haze was drifting from the sky, and the sharp emerald green of the trees blended into the pale colors of the foliage and other growth. Far in the distance, if they squinted, they could see the red tiles of the estate and the minaret of the mosque, a thin white pillar jutting out from the dark green foliage.

"Such a magnificent place and such a mystery, isn't it?" Sahil spoke softly, almost to himself.

"What is?" she asked, not sure what he was referring to.

"How your uncle found this place. I mean, in the middle of nowhere, far from where he lived or any town or village. How he managed to pick this particular spot."

Zaina then realized that she was privy to a special circle that not many visitors here were. Her uncle's backstory and his revelation were something written in books for those searching to find, not discussed at the dinner table or over cups of tea. "Oh, so you don't know how this happened, the history of Abdul Nagr?"

"What? Oh, do you mean how, as president of the engineering college, he got his students to all come and help build the house, install running water and flushing toilets? How he established a mission to invite all people of all walks of life to come and share their philosophies? This wondrous place has become a magnet of sorts for great thinkers and world leaders. I understand that."

"No, Sahil. That is something that was a result of his vision." She took a deep breath, not certain if she would be able to convey the weight of what she wanted to say to this new person, whom she had only met a few days ago. But then again, knowledge like this needed to be shared, and Sahil seemed like the one person whom she could share anything with. She had the strong feeling that it would stay as safe and sacred between them.

He put his water bottle down and looked at her directly, moving aside one stray hair from her cheek. "Then tell me. I want to know."

She took a deep breath and began at the beginning. Of the first saints, of their struggles with humanity and truth. Of the lineage of passing on the truth to those who had the courage to understand.

"Then, after meeting with the various Sufi leaders and gaining as much knowledge from books and sheikhs, he disconnected from the world. It was years ago. As a young man, Babajan retreated into the woods for a long period of time. His path to spiritual awakening began there.

"And then, towards the end, he had the dream. The dream of his mentor coming to him in a sea of white light, guiding him to a path of further enlightenment. He was told that he will build a community where he must share his knowledge and spread the word. The spirit of love for all humanity, in all forms and faiths.

"The mentor pointed in the distance to the mountain ahead. He asked my uncle to look closely and see the large letter *Y* carved into the mountain. 'Over there,' he was told, 'is where you will create your haven. It will be a sanctuary for peace.' My uncle understood then that his life was not his own, that he was in service to a greater calling. Can you see the *Y* in the mountain, Sahil?"

Her voice was soft and melodic. She pointed straight ahead. It was visible right there before them. He had been looking at it all this time, but until she had pointed it out, he never knew it was there. He looked and was taken aback as to how clearly the shape of the letter *Y* came into view.

"The great why of why we are here on earth, of why certain paths are taken or forced upon us. All the questions of the universe are there. There is no answer. The answer is the why. Until we question our existence and seek knowledge to find the truth, we remain slaves to this earthly world. It's up to us to find and seek our purpose for coming into this world."

She got up then. "Let's go back now. Someone will be sending out a search party soon if we don't."

Sahil got up, but something had shifted in his mind. First, the encounter with Babajan, and now Zaina and the history of this place. Something was happening to him. This new awakening meant that life would never be the same again.

Acknowledgments

I would like to offer my gratitude to so many people who have been there on my journey, as at this stage in my life, this would simply not have been possible without their support and love.

The Bethesda Writers Center, where I found my voice and purpose through the amazing workshops, classes, writers' groups, and mentors. To my soul sisters and Goddesses Book Club, you know who you are, thank you for making it through with me all these years. Your appreciation and honesty pushed me forward to this point. To my siblings, our shared history and journeys took many paths, but all led us to that place we know as home. To my husband and children, you have taught me courage and resilience and have always been my inspiration, forever and today. And last to my Ariana and Kyran, the joy and laughter you have brought to my life breathe through me to keep me alive and creative.

About the Author

The author has a bachelor's degree in applied design from the University of Maryland. She has worked in the field of interior design for most of her career while pursuing classes and workshops in literature and creative writing, both locally and internationally. She has grown up in the Washington, DC area and has traveled back to her home country of Pakistan regularly as well as India, where her parents originated from. She spent many summers of her youth going to the Swat Valley with her family. She has been published in the *Washington Post* and has written several essays and short stories. She currently resides in Virginia with her family. This is her first novel.

Milton Keynes UK
Ingram Content Group UK Ltd.
UKHW022355080324
439162UK00004B/195